THE QUIET KEPT

A Novel
by Claire Rowan

Published by Rowan House Publishing.

First edition.

CHAPTER ONE—THE ROAD BACK

The road to the farm hasn't changed. Two lanes. Cracked. Patched. Clay shoulders pulled tight against the winter fields. Pines leaning in at the same angle they always have. The fences still sag like tired men after Sunday service—holding on because holding on is what they know.

I drive with both hands on the wheel. Loose, not gripping. Roads behave better when you don't try to correct them. The tires hum. The land unwinds. Something settles under my ribs. Not pain. Memory fitting itself back into the body.

My mother sits in the passenger seat. Hands folded. Quiet. She watches the trees, not the road. She doesn't need to speak to be understood.

Mae sits behind her, forehead against the window, breathing fog onto the glass. She doesn't draw shapes this time. Her reflection overlaps mine—older, sharper. She just watches.

My father sits behind me. He murmurs to the land the way some people talk to gravestones.

"Used to be a feed store there," he says, almost to himself.

We don't answer. There's nothing to add. The windshield holds a dull reflection of the gravel lot.

"It's not safe out here," my mother says eventually. "Never was."

I nod. "I know."

The trees break for a moment—a thin run of ditch and dormant pasture. Something flashes across the headlights—too fast, too upright, too wrong. I tap the brakes before I understand why.

Dad leans forward. "Deer," he says, settling back.

But deer don't move like that.

He clears his throat once, a small catch in the hymn he was humming, as if something brushed past him too.

The air folds cold across my chest, a brief pressure under my sternum.

Mae lifts her head. "What was that?"

"Nothing," I say. But the road feels changed, like something stepped out of it and stayed behind.

A faint pull gathers at the base of my skull—there and gone—like the air shifted a second too late.

We booked the house like strangers.

But the truth is, it didn't start with the reservation.

Weeks earlier, I opened an old cardboard box and found a thin high-school anthology with my farm story printed inside, pages yellowed soft at the edges. I handed it to Sam that night. His voice caught on the final lines—the way it never does. Something in me shifted then. Quiet but certain. The past had already begun its pull long before we typed the dates.

A reservation link. A lock code. A message signed with no history.

The town is called something different now—**Fletcher's Grove,** polished and pluralized for maps and listings. The house has a name softened for tourists. People like new names when they don't want to know what came before.

"We could still turn back," Mae says.

"We're already here," I say.

She lets the sentence settle. Doesn't push it further.

The sky hangs low—metallic, dull with cold. Weather coming. Cold that settles and stays.

My father hums a hymn without realizing. Light. Steady. He looks out the window the way he used to look at the lake in late afternoon. Like something in him remembers itself here.

We pass the church. Fresh paint. New siding. Same bell.

My mother's jaw tightens once. That's enough to say everything.

"It's good we came," Mae says. Her voice is soft, like she's laying a blanket over something that might break if exposed too quickly.

I don't answer at first. The truth has weight. Name it too loudly and it crushes the room.

"It is," I say.

The turn appears when it always has—sudden and familiar. I slow and take the gravel road. The car shifts from pavement to stone. Pines rise in a corridor on either side.

No one speaks.

We crest the small hill and the house appears.

Roofline first. Then porch. Then windows that used to hold warm dusk like a held breath.

My chest pulls tight. Not sadness. Recognition.

"It's smaller," Mae says.

"Everything is," I say.

We step out into the cold. It finds the seams in coats, the space between ribs. It smells like woodsmoke, frozen earth, and something old opening its eyes.

My father stands still, hands at his sides. His eyes shine, but not in a way that needs comment.

My mother touches the railing with two fingertips. Like greeting a grave she isn't ready to stand at.

I take the steps. The boards give the way they always did. I set my hand on the post. The wood remembers us.

I key in the lock code.

The keypad chirps. The latch gives.

The house exhales. A thin draft lifts against my skin, colder than the wind outside.

For one moment—one breath held between now and before—it feels like nothing ever left.

Then the wind shifts.

Iron-cold slides in under the doorframe. Sharpened. Intentional. Not weather.

Something else.

Aware.

Someone is waiting.

CHAPTER TWO—WARMTH

The warmth meets us first. Not heat—just the shape of the rooms, familiar in a way I can't name.

Something in the air pushes up against me—like a thought spoken too close—and without meaning to, I smooth it down the way you quiet a skittish horse—with a palm, not a word. A habit I don't remember learning.

The same open line of sight from the front door to the kitchen.

Someone has cleaned and painted. It doesn't matter. The bones haven't changed.

I exhale without meaning to.

Mae does too. "It smells right," she says.

Wood. Damp corners. Coffee that isn't from today.

She sets her bag down, then lifts it again. "I'm just going to—"

Something in her hesitates, and I feel it before I name it.

"Go," I say. "I'll get the rest."

My mother stands still, looking at nothing. Her shoulders lift once, barely, like the weight shifts and returns. Regret has a posture.

My father lowers himself onto the couch facing the fireplace. His hands rest on his lap.

"Unbelievable," he says. Quiet. Almost a prayer.

I take two more trips to the car. The cold is sharp, clean, familiar.

When I return, Mae is in our old room. I push the door open with my foot.

She has already unpacked the real essentials:

Two glasses wrapped in towels. A Ziploc of ice. A small bottle without a label.

She doesn't have to explain.

"Good call," I say.

"Sit," she says.

I do.

She pours. The ice cracks. We lift our glasses without ceremony.

The first swallow is too strong. We both make the face. Then we laugh—quiet, relief, and disbelief.

"I didn't think we'd actually come," she says.

"Maybe we shouldn't have."

"Probably not."

We sit on the edge of the bed, knees touching. The room is quiet in the way old rooms are—holding every sound instead of echoing it.

We finish the drinks. Not fast. Not slow.

I set my glass down and notice the gouge in the nightstand where a knot once was. The owners redecorated, but the house didn't forget.

"Ready?" I ask.

"No," she says, standing. "But okay."

We follow the hallway. The light here is warm. Softer than before.

The owners have hung framed photographs.

We stop.

It's the house. The porch. Our family.

PaPa with one arm around my father. My mother's careful smile. Mae, hair in a thin pony. Me, white-blonde and squinting.

And the boy.

Barefoot. Twelve or fourteen. Hand resting on the porch rail like he lived in that gesture.

Something tightens in my chest. Not grief. Memory without shape.

"I don't remember him," I say.

Something in my insides pulls—not fear, just recognition without a name.

Mae watches the photograph a long time before answering.

"He used to fish with PaPa," she says. "Down at the lake."

The feeling makes sense—not as memory, but as something carried long before I could name it.

The word settles.

My father's reflection appears in the glass. His gaze finds the boy and does not move on.

"We were told he drowned," Mae says, barely audible.

We were told a lot of things.

I look at the boy's hand on the railing. As if the house itself remembers differently.

Mae touches my wrist. "Come on," she says.

We go to the kitchen.

The room has been updated, but not changed. Same layout. Same hooks for mugs.

A second drink was sneakily poured—Mae and I sip, cook, and giggle quietly; standard, easy-to-travel chili ingredients simmer on the stovetop, forgiving and familiar. My father places bowls on the table. Crackers. Butter. No rush.

"Time to eat," my mother says.

We sit.

The meal is quiet in the right way. Spoons. Steam.

My father tells a story about raccoon hunting with the pastor. He laughs softly. My mother allows herself a smile.

Mae's shoulders loosen.

Mine do too, though I don't acknowledge it.

"It's good that we came," Mae says.

"It is," I say.

And in this moment, it is.

We clear the table.

My father carries bowls. My mother pretends not to watch his balance. I wash. Mae dries.

I take the trash outside. The cold wakes the blood.

When I return to the living room, the shape of heat has shifted.

Not gone. Just tipped off center. Something is different.

A thin thread of cold moves through my insides, like the room is bracing for something before I am.

I stop in the doorway.

Mae bumps me lightly—then stops too.

Dara is sitting in PaPa's recliner.

She is upright. Hands folded. Legs crossed at the ankle. Cheek angled toward the fire like she belongs to the house more than we do.

Her hair is box-dye black. Her lipstick too red. Her skin winter-pale.

"Hi," she says, without turning. "I thought I'd save you the trouble of inviting me."

Mae goes quiet. I feel my chest tighten.

Dara lifts her head and looks at me first. Her expression is not warm. Not cruel. Just certain.

"It's been a long time," she says.

"It has," I answer.

She stands slowly. Deliberately.

The house holds still.

She crosses the room and sits in my father's seat at the head of the table—the one closest to the fireplace.

The place of authority. Inheritance. Memory.

She places her hands on the table.

"Why are we all here?" she asks.

Her tone is not a question.

It's accusation. Expectation. Premonition.

My mother sets down dessert without looking at her. She sits two places away.

My father stands a moment longer than necessary, then takes a chair beside my mother instead of reclaiming his place.

"We were telling old stories," he says.

Dara leans back, satisfied.

"Good," she says. "Those are my favorite."

The heater shuts off.

The room cools by a single degree.

Comfort moves first.

Then the truth.

Dara does not sleep the way other people do.

She goes to bed because the body expects it, because the hour demands it, because routines are useful even when rest is optional. But her mind stays upright—alert, arranging, attentive to what has not yet happened but already exists in outline.

Her house is quiet in the way places become when no one is coming home later. No doors waiting to be opened. No footsteps that might interrupt. The silence here is earned, not tentative.

A single lamp burns in the kitchen, its shade tilted low. Outside, winter presses up against the windows, testing for gaps. Dara barely registers it. Weather is only interesting when it can be used.

She sets her phone on the table and wakes it without ceremony. The glow is soft, controlled. Brightness dialed down, notifications silenced. She has never liked devices that announce themselves.

The listing opens where she left it.

It sits there like something already owned.

The photographs come first. Wide shots meant to reassure. Corners trimmed away. A kitchen brightened by lamps placed deliberately out of frame. A living room arranged to look generous rather than accurate. A hallway that seems to recede farther than it should, suggesting space where space will be noticed.

Dara scrolls slowly—not savoring, measuring.

She looks at photographs the way some people look at blueprints. What matters is not what is shown, but what is omitted.

No photograph of the back door from the outside. No clear image of the yard at night. No angle facing uphill.

Absence is not an error. It is a decision, even if the person making it doesn't know why.

She taps the host profile.

The smiling couple appears again. Teeth too white. Flannel folded just right. The sort of practiced warmth people mistake for sincerity. Their eyes catch the light wrong—too reflective, as if the flash bounced back instead of going in.

Dara enlarges the image and holds it until the faces dissolve into grain.

Not because she wants to see them better.

Because she likes the way clarity breaks down when you insist on too much of it.

She opens the message thread—already familiar.

So glad you're staying with us! If there's a storm, don't worry. Emergency supplies in the small outbuilding. Kerosene lamps. Extra fuel. A small generator if needed.

Dara reads the lines again.

Not for reassurance. For structure.

Scripts are useful. People follow them when pressure arrives.

She scrolls to the access information.

Gate code. Parking. The narrow gravel lane that looks like it goes nowhere if you don't already know where it leads.

She memorizes it without trying.

Then she taps the calendar.

Availability tells its own story. Weekends clustered around holidays. Long winter gaps. A handful of midweek bookings that look local—people who know which nights are quiet, which times no one checks.

She watches the dates form a pattern.

Some patterns are chosen. Some are inherited. Both are exploitable.

She checks the address again—not for directions, but for distances.

How far the nearest neighbor sits. How long sound would carry in cold air. How quickly help could arrive if someone believed it needed to.

She is not planning an emergency.

She is removing interruptions.

Four adults. One property. Weather that encourages patience and excuses.

The calculation is clean.

Her thumb pauses at *House Rules*.

No parties. No smoking. Quiet hours after ten.

She exhales once—not laughter. Recognition.

People like this believe rules create safety simply because they exist. They hang crosses above outbuildings. They call it blessing. They believe naming something means controlling it.

Dara opens the emergency note again. The one about the shed. The lamps. The generator.

She reads it twice.

Then she returns to the photos and enlarges the yard. Snow softens the ground in the picture, makes everything appear forgiving. In the far background, barely present, a dark lift that could be trees or hill or fence.

Dara drags her finger across the screen, enlarging until the image fractures.

She doesn't need detail.

She needs shape.

It rises.

Everything out there rises.

She exits the listing and opens her notes app.

A short list waits for her—unembellished, efficient:

— Storm window

— Outbuilding

— Power

— Isolation

— Who arrives / who doesn't

She reads the last line again.

Who arrives / who doesn't.

Claire will believe she's managing this by bringing everyone together. Claire always thinks proximity solves something—that if people share air and table and rooms, coherence will eventually follow.

Dara has never believed that.

Proximity doesn't heal.

It concentrates.

That is what makes it useful.

She sets the phone down and watches the lamp's glow pool against the table. The house around her makes no comment. It has learned her habits. It knows better than to interrupt.

She opens a browser and skims weather reports. Road advisories. Notices about outages farther north. Warnings phrased gently so people don't overreact.

Winter systems moving faster than expected. Gusts. Possible outages.

The kind of trouble people like to blame on the sky.

She opens the map next and zooms until lines become roads, then lanes, then nothing at all. She traces the route the way one might trace a scar—not to understand it, but to remember exactly where it lies.

Where headlights will throw. Where they won't. Where a car can sit without being seen.

Orientation matters.

When she closes the apps, the kitchen feels momentarily too still, as if the room has noticed the absence of light and is waiting to see what comes next.

Dara stands, crosses to the counter, and opens a drawer.

From it, she takes a small notebook and tears a clean strip from the edge.

She writes one sentence.

Not a plan. Not a confession.

A boundary.

Don't let them make it ordinary.

She sets the paper face down and slides it beneath the notebook, as if even objects can overhear when left exposed.

When she turns off the lamp, she does it without pause.

The dark does not trouble her.

She moves through her own hallway with certainty, closes her bedroom door, and lies down. The house accepts her weight without complaint.

This time, she lets her eyes close.

Not because she's tired.

Because nothing remains undecided.

Everyone else will travel. They will pack. They will talk. They will believe the trip is still unfolding.

Dara has already been where they are going.

The choice has been made.

Now she only has to wait for the others to arrive inside it.

CHAPTER THREE — MORNING

The house feels different in the morning. Not warm, not inviting—just rested, as if it had been holding its breath through the night and finally let it go. Light pushes in through the long wall of windows, pale and thin, catching dust in the air and the quiet edges of everything.

My mother sits in the living room near the fireplace with a cup of tea. She isn't reading. Just resting her hands around the mug, her gaze fixed somewhere past the flames.

My father is at the table, coffee held in both hands. He blows across the surface once before taking a slow, careful sip. He has always taken his time with mornings. His thumb taps his wedding band—a small, familiar motion I almost miss.

Mae and I come in quietly, like we've stepped into a room where something delicate is being stitched back together.

Something in my chest tightens before I can smooth it down.

Dara is already seated at the table.

A shift moves through me—subtle, off. Not danger. Not yet. Just wrong.

Her back is straight. Shoulders lifted, rigid, as if her body forgot how to rest even while sitting. Her hair is the same box-dye black under the morning light, too matte, too heavy. Her lipstick is smeared at the edge of her mouth—not fresh, not slept-in. Just wrong.

Her coffee sits untouched in front of her. No steam. Cold.

She stares straight ahead, past the table, past the glass, into the long stretch of windows and the frost-laced land beyond. Not watching anything. Gone somewhere. Not catatonic. Not dramatic. Just empty in a way that doesn't ask to be noticed.

No one speaks to her.

There are bowls of oatmeal on the table—already beginning to cool. My mother must have made it earlier, quietly, the way she always did. If you didn't come when it was ready, you ate it lukewarm.

That was the rule. Not spoken—just understood.

Mae and I take our bowls.

We don't fill the silence. We don't acknowledge Dara.

The distance is old, familiar, worn smooth.

I take a bite. Plain. Soft. It tastes like every winter morning we ever had here—where warmth wasn't something the house gave you. You made it yourself and held on as long as you could.

No one says how they slept. No one asks.

When the bowls are scraped mostly clean and the quiet stretches thin, I stand. Mae stands with me. Our coats wait by the door.

I glance at my parents—just enough that they understand we'll be back, that nothing is wrong, that nothing needs saying.

"We'll be back."

My father nods once.

My mother doesn't look away from the fire.

Dara doesn't move.

Outside, the cold is sharper than yesterday. Our breaths cloud the air. Frost webs the window corners—delicate patterns that will vanish when the sun climbs a little higher.

Mae pulls her coat tighter. She doesn't speak, but I know what she's thinking: the lake. The hill. The way this land holds memory.

We walk.

Gravel crunches under our boots. The air wakes the skin. The house shrinks behind us, quiet and still, as though listening.

The air feels heavier near the windows, like something inside the house notices us leaving.

We pass the pond that isn't really a pond—the lake that held every summer of our childhoods. Its surface is still. Too still.

A faint tug moves low inside me—the kind that comes before a memory or a warning. I can't tell which. Like the hush that followed the traveling pastor's fire-and-brimstone sermons—the kind that made you afraid of being alive the wrong way.

I think of the Wonder Bread bags our mother slid over our shoes in winter when we were small. Shoes, then bags, then rubber bands at the ankles to keep the cold out. People probably thought it was pointless.

It worked. Or at least, I remember that it did.

It felt like care.

We reach the base of the hill.

The haunted house sits just beyond the trees, though we can't see it yet.

We stop at the same time.

Not because of fear. Because we remember everything here.

Branches shift behind us.

Mae and I turn.

Dara stands a few yards back, arms wrapped tight around her coat, hair stirring slightly in the cold breeze. She must have followed without a sound.

The breeze skims my skin, cold moving against the direction of the wind.

She tilts her head, her voice slipping into that strange, sweet, childlike tone—the one that never belonged to her at any age.

"This is fun," she says softly. Almost sing-song. "Just like when we were little."

Her smile is small.

Wrong. Too gentle.

"I've always wanted to come back up here with you two."

A beat.

"Be careful where you step."

She says it like she's remembering something we haven't remembered yet.

The hill waits. The house waits.

The past doesn't stay buried just because we stopped saying its name.

CHAPTER FOUR — THE THRESHOLD

We don't choose the moment we move. It chooses us.

The snow has stopped pretending to glitter. It lies dull and thin over ruts and roots, as if it knows more about the day than we do. The air is colder than last night; it has the careful feeling of church before anyone speaks.

Dara stands on the porch, turned toward the dark opening where the door should be. She isn't inspecting anything. She's just there—still, fixed—as if the house is reading her.

Mae's fingers rest at my wrist the way they did when we were little: Sunday bench, shoes too tight, chin up, don't let your face tell on you. She isn't nervous so much as tender. I can feel her mourning the past and trying not to show it.

I have my own method. I think about small things: the way oatmeal skins if you don't stir it; the squeak our old screen door made in summer; the tiny seam that used to run down the back of PaPa's dress pants—almost invisible, but my eyes always found it.

It keeps me here.

Dara's voice returns in that child tone, the one that doesn't belong in any adult mouth.

"C'mon," she sings softly. "This is fun."

She lifts her hand into the empty doorway but doesn't cross it. Her palm hovers over the dark, as if feeling for temperature.

"Careful where you step," she adds sweetly—high and wrong.

Then the voice drops flat. "Or don't."

Mae's touch tightens. "We don't have to do this," she says. It isn't fear. It's love.

I nod once, which means everything and nothing.

Then I step forward—one board, then another. The wood gives a long, tired sound. The porch sags and holds. A quiet awareness gathers around us, nothing sharp—just present.

Up close I can see where a rail once was: empty mortises, rust stains like old tears along the post. Time took it, or something else did. It doesn't matter. It's gone.

The doorway carries the familiar trace—old wood, wet paper, mouse.

It is the opposite of the kitchen at home, where Sam leaves oranges in a bowl by the sink. For a moment I picture those oranges, bright and clean. Then I let them go.

Inside, the light is thin. The front room is smaller than memory, and the realization settles deeper than I expect.

The bones are the same: one window on the left, another straight ahead, both filmed with grime; floorboards wide enough for a child's foot to slip between; a stove that isn't a stove anymore—just a shape against the wall. Wallpaper is gone except where scraps cling high in a corner like the last guests at a party that ended years ago.

We don't speak. The room would notice.

Mae steps beside me. Not in front. Not behind. Beside. She studies the sill, the way water has flaked the paint into curled crescents. Her eyes shine—not tears, just that old ache that doesn't announce itself.

The floor is cool under my steps. A shiver climbs without asking.

Dara follows last. She crosses the threshold without looking down, as if rules don't apply to her. The baby voice is gone. She's quiet now—blank, absent—a body held up by strings.

She moves to the far window and stands too close to the rotten frame, staring at nothing, breathing softly like she's afraid of disturbing something she wants awake.

"Don't lean," I say.

She doesn't answer.

I test the floor with my weight. The boards speak old-limb noises. In the corner near the baseboard: a shooter marble, dirty with age, blue glass dulled but not broken.

I don't pick it up. I let it stay where it belongs.

We move deeper, slow. A narrow hall. Then the angle of the stairs. The first step is a different wood— replaced once, badly—then rises up, all shallow and mean.

Newspaper peels from the wall along the stairwell and the landing above: headlines from a world that believed itself new. 1912. 1908. Prices for flour and salt. A traveling tent revival set for the third Sunday. A boy with a cowlick selling seed for pocket change.

The paper is brown and crisp, clinging like something that knows how to hold on.

Mae breathes out, quiet. "It's still here," she says. She means the dates. She means us.

The wind presses at the house and the house answers with a low, patient sound. It threads through the walls, steady as breath. Not mine. Not Mae's. Tired.

I feel the weight of all the winters it has carried without anyone to speak for it.

"We don't go up," I say.

Mae nods. She already made the same decision.

Dara doesn't move. Her hands hang at her sides, fingers still. She stares at the stairwell without blinking, as if waiting for a picture to form out of empty air.

"Do you remember," she says suddenly—normal voice, wrong content—"how he used to run ahead?"

Mae freezes, just long enough for me to feel her thinking.

"Who," Mae asks. The word is small.

"The boy," Dara says, as if she's telling us something kind. "He liked these stairs." She tilts her head, unfocused. "He liked to pretend the landing was a stage."

Cold spreads through me, then thins again.

I remember a barefoot boy holding a porch rail in a photograph I didn't recognize. I remember being told he drowned. I remember adults choosing sentences that close doors.

"We should go," I say.

Dara turns to me. Her eyes are almost black in the poor light. She opens her mouth, as if the baby voice might return, then shuts it.

Flat, she says, "He didn't drown."

The house listens.

Mae's hand finds my sleeve and holds.

"We're not doing this here," I say. Steady.

Dara looks back to the stairwell, her expression smoothed into something too practiced to be natural.

"He fell," she says softly, more to the wall than to us.

Then the voice thins, drifting toward that child lilt. "Unless someone helped."

Mae's breath catches—once, just enough for me to hear.

I feel the useless urge to fix something no one can fix—to tighten a screw, straighten a picture, stir the oatmeal before it skins.

I hold still instead.

"We're leaving," I say.

I step backward into the front room. The board beneath my heel gives a long, shivering groan.

By the window, a nail head shines through dust, bright as a small star. It's nothing. It's a nail.

But the thought arrives before logic—uninvited, precise. For a second my mind offers the shape of a boy's hand, small and dirty, reaching for balance. Or a dare. Or someone's attention.

I close my eyes and let it pass reminding myself not to argue with what the brain throws out to keep you upright.

Mae moves with me, careful, grief-soft.

We stand in the doorway and let the outside air reach our faces. It tastes cleaner than it did a minute ago.

Dara doesn't follow.

She remains by the stairwell, head tipped, body quiet as a second thought. The baby voice leaks out in a single line, almost tender.

"We used to be brave."

I step onto the porch. The board holds.

The field beyond is pale and patient. The trees keep their counsel.

"We were children," I say—not loud, not to her. "We were just children."

We wait—Mae at my shoulder, my breath slow and visible—until Dara looks at us again.

The expression on her face isn't anger. It isn't grief. It's simpler. Calculation with a coating of sweetness.

She smiles a small, neat smile that never reaches her eyes.

"Okay," she says brightly. "We'll go."

She chooses the threshold as if nothing was said. She passes between us, onto the porch—one careful step, then another.

She doesn't look back at the house. She doesn't look at us.

She walks into the thin snow and heads toward the trees.

Mae lets go of my sleeve. The place where her fingers were feels warmer than the rest of me.

Behind us, the house keeps standing—tired, patient, full of what it has kept. Wind works along the eaves, slips through a seam, and makes a low whistle.

It isn't a warning. It isn't a welcome. It's a reminder.

Some truths don't chase you. They wait where you left them and make you come back the long way.

We step down into the snow and follow the path Dara is already making.

No one speaks.

The day moves with us, quiet as prayer.

CHAPTER FIVE — THE RETURNING

Night falls early here. Not quickly—just inevitably. Dark that seeps, not drops. The house doesn't fight it. It receives it the way old barns receive rain: with familiarity, not resistance.

We've been back for only one full day, but the air has already thickened the way it used to. Not heavy. Just aware. Like the house has woken to listen.

Mae and I sit in the living room with the lights low. The fireplace crackles the way it always has—slow, uneven, never quite enough heat to do more than keep your hands flexible.

My mother is somewhere down the hall. My father has gone to bed. Or to pray. Hard to know the difference in him now.

Dara stands at the window.

She hasn't spoken since we left the old house on the hill. Not a word. Her hands rest lightly on the sill, as if she's waiting to feel something through it. A pulse. A memory. A return.

Mae watches her, quietly. I do too.

The silence is familiar—but not comforting.

"Do you remember," Dara says finally, so soft I almost miss it, "how the nights sounded here?"

Mae shakes her head. "Not really."

Dara smiles—small, thin, unkind.

"You do," she says. "You just don't want to."

Outside, something shifts in the tree line.

Not movement.

Recognition.

A pause in the dark—something adjusting to our presence.

I stand. "Let's not do this tonight."

Dara's reflection in the glass lifts her chin slightly. She doesn't turn.

"Do what?"

"This," I say. "Whatever this is."

Dara exhales. The window fogs in a small oval.

"I didn't bring this with me," she says. "It was already here."

Mae looks at me. I look back.

We don't argue.

The house pops and settles. The wind presses once at the eaves—a long, slow sound, almost like breath.

Dara steps back from the window and turns, expression smooth, eyes glass-dark.

"He remembers us," she says.

My stomach goes cold in that slow, blooming way the body reserves for truths you've already known and refused.

Mae's voice thins. "Who?"

Dara tilts her head gently, like the question belongs to a child.

"The boy."

There is no dramatic silence—not here.

Just the house receiving the sentence and holding it.

I sit again. My hands are steady. My breath is not.

"No one is remembering anything tonight," I say.

Dara blinks. Then again. Her face softens, which is somehow worse than anything sharp.

"You were always so good at shutting doors," she says. "Even when you were little."

Mae stands too fast. "Enough."

Dara smiles. Not wide. Not cruel. Just certain.

"We don't get to choose what comes back."

The fire flickers low.

The warmth thins.

The night folds itself closer.

My mother enters then—quiet, composed, carrying blankets.

She places one beside me. One beside Mae.

None near Dara.

"We should sleep," she says.

No argument.

No explanation.

Just the rule.

We take what's ours and move down the hall.

The living room remains behind us, dim and patient.

In my room, I sit on the edge of the bed and unwrap the blanket. It smells like cedar and storage and the long-ago summers when all we knew and loved was enough.

Mae stands in the doorway.

"She's not lying," she says.

I look up.

"About which part?"

Mae swallows. "The remembering."

I nod. Once. Slow.

The truth waits in the dark like something with patience.

CHAPTER SIX — THE LAKE

The morning comes slow. Not with light first, but with temperature—something settles in the bones before a person's eyes open.

I wake without remembering sleep, the way you wake in hospitals or guest rooms or childhood bedrooms you don't call yours anymore.

The house is quiet in the wrong way. Not resting. Listening.

I pull on my coat and boots without turning on the light. The hallway feels longer than it did last night, though I know it's the same number of steps.

The living room is empty. The blankets we left behind are folded again. My mother's doing. She has always cleaned the evidence of existence before daylight can catch it.

The door clicks softly behind me.

Outside, the cold is honest—sharp, clean, a small truth against the skin.

I follow the path without thinking—muscle memory from a past I never gave permission to stay.

The lake sits where it always has, as if time has been circling it instead of moving forward.

The surface is still. Not frozen—just waiting.

The trees lean toward it. Not protective. Just close.

I stop at the edge, the mud stiff with frost beneath my boots. I remember summers—bare feet, minnows, sunlight on water—but the remembering feels distant, like watching someone else's film.

Something in me shifts. Not realization. Not memory. Acceptance.

This land knows us whether we claim it or not.

Footsteps approach behind me, slow and soft— someone who didn't want to be heard.

Mae.

She stands beside me, coat zipped unevenly, hair tied back loosely like she left her room without checking a mirror. She doesn't speak. She doesn't have to.

The lake gives back only sky.

She breathes once, steadying. "I used to think he lived here," she says.

The sentence is so quiet it could pass for an exhale.

I keep my eyes on the water. "Who?"

Mae's jaw tightens. "You know who."

We stand there together—sisters, daughters, children of a place that remembers more than we do.

The cold works its way through our coats.

Somewhere behind us, the house waits. Not calling. Not pulling. Patient.

"Do you think," Mae says carefully, her voice thinned with old tenderness, "we're here to remember... or to learn what we misremembered?"

I let the question rest between us like a hand placed gently on a table.

"We'll find out," I say.

Not a promise. Not fear. Truth.

The lake holds the sky, unmoving.

We stay until the cold tells us to return.

We walk back slowly, not speaking. The chill settles into our coats and the small spaces beneath our ribs. By the time the house comes back into view, the sun has climbed only a few degrees—just enough to turn frost into a thin, glassy sheen.

Inside, the air is warmer but not welcoming.

My mother stands at the sink, rinsing a mug she hasn't used. My father sits at the table with his coffee, elbows planted, mug cradled in both hands like he's holding the table hostage until he's finished. He taps the rim twice with his right index finger—once, then again—before he drinks.

Neither of them looks at us.

Mae hangs her coat on the same hook she used as a child. I do the same. The motion is quiet, practiced, as if the years between then and now have collapsed into something the house can hold in a single breath.

No one asks where we went. No one asks what we saw.

Dara is not in the room. Or in any room we can see.

The house settles once—low, patient.

The day continues.

We do our chores without naming them. I wipe the counters. Mae folds blankets no one unfolded. My father checks the woodpile. My mother moves through the kitchen with the careful grace of someone holding a memory at bay.

No one mentions the lake.

When night comes, it does not surprise us. It simply arrives, familiar as an old hymn.

We go to our rooms earlier than we intend. The house goes quiet—but not still.

And then—

Night reveals what day only softened.

32

CHAPTER SEVEN — THE HALLWAY

I wake before I know I've woken. Not with a jolt. Not from a dream. Just the waking where the body comes up first and the mind follows later.

The room is dark. Not full dark—just the washed winter blue that comes when the moon is low and the snow outside reflects whatever light remains in the sky.

I don't move.

Something is happening in the hallway.

Not sound, exactly. Not footsteps. Just weight.

A shift of the floorboards—the way old houses respond to presence—slow, careful settling under someone moving without hurry.

My door is cracked, the way it always was when we slept here as children. Not wide enough to see anything. Just wide enough to let the hallway breathe with the room.

Another shift.

Another slow, thoughtful step.

I keep my breath even.

Quiet. Aware.

Mae and I used to do this—lie still and listen—when the adults whispered down the hall after late church nights. When the words weren't meant for us. When the house seemed to know more than it should.

A third step.

The weight is wrong.

Not heavy like my father's gait. Not soft like my mother's. Not the floating quiet of Mae.

This is a step placed with memory of the house. Of which boards speak. Of which ones hold.

Someone who has walked here before.

The hallway settles again—closer this time.

I think of Wonder Bread bags around our feet. I think of Sam's oranges in a ceramic bowl. I think of the lake in summer heat. The picture of the boy with his hand on the porch rail.

I don't move.

The door shifts—just slightly.

Not pushed. Just… responding.

Like someone has stopped in front of it and the air has changed.

The house holds its breath.

So do I.

A voice moves through the crack—soft, too close, too familiar in the wrong way:

"Are you awake?"

Not Dara's child voice. Not her practiced polite one.

Something quieter. Almost careful. Almost gentle.

Mae rests peacefully. Not making a sound.

I don't answer.

The voice waits.

One beat. Two.

Then, almost tender:

"You always pretended you didn't hear me."

The floorboard eases under that remembered weight—and then moves away.

Slow. Even. Down the hall.

The house releases its breath.
I let mine go with it.
I don't close the door.
Not yet.

CHAPTER EIGHT — THE GRAVE

The sky has the color of washed tin.

We drive without speaking. The road is familiar in the way old hymns are—learned young, never forgotten, even when the meaning slips away.

My father keeps both hands on the wheel, though the wind isn't strong and the road doesn't require it. My mother sits straight, her coat zipped to the throat. Mae watches the fields. I watch the way the fence posts lean.

No one says where we're going.

We turn by the church—fresh siding, new roof, bright white sign announcing service times in clean block letters. Too new. Too proud. It stands wrong against the land, like someone dressing grief in a party dress.

The cemetery is small. The same way it always was. Grass thin. Gravel patchwork. Trees bare and still.

The cold here is steady, not biting—something that has settled and made a home.

My father kills the engine. The quiet after it stops is immediate.

We get out.

Boots on gravel. Breath in air that tastes of iron and earth.

No instructions. No hesitation.

We walk.

The path bends once, gentle. My father leads without meaning to. My mother keeps a careful pace. Mae walks close beside me, shoulder brushing mine once, then again.

We reach the stone.

Small. Plain. Not child-small. Just… unadorned.

No flowers. No dates that matter.

Just a name we were taught not to say out loud.

And on top—

A stack of stones.

Rounded. Weather-soft. Placed one at a time.

Years of visits. Years of grief kept quiet.

Mae inhales sharply. Not a sob. Something smaller. Quieter. Older.

My father steps forward. His hat is in his hands. He lowers his head. He stands in stillness that is not prayer and not memory—just presence.

My mother stays a step back, as if closeness might break something in her she cannot fix.

The cold moves through the grass.

I look at the stones. One on another. Balanced. Tender. A language older than apology.

PaPa did this.

For years. Maybe decades.

While we lived our lives believing the story that made everything easier to bear.

Mae touches my wrist, gentle.

"We knew him," she says.

My mother closes her eyes.

Not long. Just enough for the truth to move through her before she opens them again.

My father places one more stone on the stack.

His hand shakes.

Not much. Just enough to see.

The air shifts. Not wind. Something remembered.

I see—not clearly, not in full—

Sunlight. Porch rail. Bare feet dusty to the ankle. Mae humming. A dare. A laugh too loud for quiet hours.

A fall that wasn't meant to happen.

Or was. Or wasn't. Or can't be named at all.

The memory pulls tight, then loosens before I can touch it.

I step back.

The land holds its silence.

We turn toward the gravel path without deciding to.

No one looks back.

The walk to the car is slow. Not heavy. Just careful, like the ground might break if we move too quickly.

When we reach the car—

Dara is already inside.

Back seat. Hands folded. Face calm. No coat.

She must have followed.

Or she was already here.

Or there are things we have stopped trying to understand.

She looks at Mae first. Then me.

A small, soft smile—almost tender.

"You remembered," she says.

Not accusation. Not triumph. Just certainty.

No one answers.

The cold settles around us, patient.

The engine starts.

The stones stay.

The day goes on.

CHAPTER NINE — THE BIBLE COVER

We aren't looking for anything when we find it.

Mae is sorting the linen closet—old towels, blankets that smell like cedar and storage, sheets from a bed that isn't here anymore. I hand things down. She folds them. The work is quiet. Ordinary. The kind that feels older than we are.

Then her hand stops.

She closes her fingers around something soft but firm—vinyl, the corners stiff with age.

She brings it down.

A Bible cover.

Maroon. Zipper broken at one end.

The kind DeeDee kept close and placed strategically long after she could no longer attend church. Because this Bible cover held authority.

No one speaks.

Mae unzips it carefully, as if what's inside has temperature.

No Bible.

Just wrappers—Juicy Fruit—folded into tidy squares.

More than two dozen four-leaf clovers tucked between them.

Dozens of pieces. Smoothed. Saved.

Evidence of the clover hunts Mae had with her.

And at the bottom, a small piece of lined paper torn from a pad:

Bread (place on very top of grocery bag)
Oleo
Milk (extra for calf)
Dried beans
Ask him

Mae reads it once.

Sets it down.

We stand there in the hallway.

The morning light is thin. Dust floats in it.

The air feels like when the choir stops singing but everyone is still holding the last note inside their bodies.

"She saved everything," Mae says.

"She didn't know how to let go," I answer.

Mae nods—not in agreement, but in recognition.

"She loved him," Mae says.

The boy's father.

"Everyone knew." But knowing it now is different than knowing it then.

Then it was gossip.

Now it is evidence.

The kind that has weight.

The house seems to lean in—not listening for secrets, just remembering them.

Mae sits back on her heels.

"Do you think he knew?"

"Yes," I say.

Not because I'm sure.

But because some answers live under the skin.

She looks at the gum wrappers again—each one handled like it had meaning.

Which means it did.

"This was how she prayed," Mae says quietly.

Not only to God.

To memory.

To the hope that keeping something was the same as keeping someone.

I don't touch the Bible cover.

Some things are not meant to be handled twice.

We put the towels back.

We close the closet door.

The house settles, slow and long, like a deep exhale.

Nothing is solved. Nothing is undone.

But something has shifted.

Not in the past.

In us.

CHAPTER TEN(AON)— THE HOLDING

I don't notice the shift right away. That's the danger of things that feel familiar—they arrive wearing older clothes.

It comes as a pressure first. It comes as a pressure first. Not fear. Not memory. Something narrower. Like a room settling after someone slips out in an Irish goodbye—no acknowledgment, just absence organizing itself. The house is quiet, but not resting. It has the attentive stillness of a body braced against weather it knows is coming.

I'm wiping the counter when it happens. The cloth pauses in my hand. The air pulls tight under my ribs, then steadies—as if waiting to see what I'll do.

I smooth it without thinking. A palm to the edge of it. Not pushing back. Just laying it flat.

It works. Mostly.

The warmth doesn't leave, but it redistributes. Like heat shifting in a room where the fire has burned down to coals. Enough to keep bones from stiffening. Not enough to forget the cold exists.

Mae is in the living room. I can hear the slow drag of her footsteps across the rug, the careful way she moves when she's listening for something she won't name yet. My parents murmur in the kitchen—ordinary words, measured, chosen. Dara hasn't spoken in a while. That absence has weight.

The house responds to all of it. A small adjustment in the floorboards. A soft tick somewhere in the walls. Not warning. Accounting.

I tell myself it's memory. Old spaces warming to old bodies. The mind filling in gaps the way it always does when it returns somewhere it once learned how to survive.

But memory doesn't press back.

This does.

The feeling gathers again—low and steady—like a held breath that isn't mine. I don't name it. Naming would give it an edge. I let it sit, let it be what it is.

Containment, not control.

For a moment, the house loosens. Just enough to suggest agreement.

Then the pressure settles deeper—no longer around us, but beneath. As if something has been set down carefully and left there on purpose.

I understand then—not fully, but enough—that whatever is happening isn't arriving.

It's been holding.

And now that we're here, it's ready to see who remembers how.

CHAPTER TEN(DHÀ) — THE HOLDING

The problem with knowing how to smooth things is that you begin to believe you should.

The thought arrives quietly, the way habits do. I could press a little harder. I could move the edges in. I could name what's happening and force it back where it belongs.

The house doesn't ask me to. It just waits.

Dara shifts somewhere behind me—one chair leg scraping softly against wood. The sound lands wrong in the room, out of proportion to its size. Mae stills. I feel it before I see it, the way awareness travels faster than sight.

Nothing happens.

That's the point.

The pressure holds at a low, patient level, like it's testing the limits of courtesy. Not a threat. An invitation. The kind you're expected to answer because you always have before.

My chest tightens—not fear, not urgency— recognition. This is the place where things tip if you let them. Where responsibility disguises itself as care.

I think of all the times I learned to keep rooms calm. Church basements. Hospital waiting areas. Kitchens after arguments. You don't raise your voice. You don't name what people can't survive hearing yet. You make space and hope it's enough.

Most of the time, it was.

The Quiet in me stirs—not rising, not pushing—just alert. Like a hand hovering near a light switch, knowing exactly where it is.

I almost use it.

The impulse is clean. Reasonable. If I ease this now, everyone will sleep. My parents will sit more comfortably in their bodies. Mae won't keep watching the corners of the room. Dara will stop smiling like she's waiting for something to break.

The house would accept it. I'm certain of that.

But acceptance isn't the same as resolution. I've learned that too.

I look at the floor instead. At the long grain of the boards, the small scars time never bothered to erase. This house has carried heavier things than discomfort. It survived because someone let it remember instead of fixing it every time it started to speak.

I let my hand fall to my side.

The pressure shifts—not gone, not dulled—but adjusted, like something recalibrating its expectations. There's no approval in it. Just acknowledgment.

Dara laughs once under her breath. Not loud. Not amused. Something closer to interest.

I don't look at her.

Choosing not to act is still a choice. It has weight. It settles differently in the body than relief does.

The house knows it too.

CHAPTER TEN(TRÌ) — THE HOLDING

The house doesn't push after that.

It settles into a different posture—still attentive, but no longer testing me. The air eases by degrees, not enough to feel like relief. Enough to feel decided. Whatever line I refused to cross stays where it is.

Sound becomes clearer once the pressure shifts. The tick in the walls resolves into heat traveling through old pipes. Wind threads the eaves and finds a loose place to worry, making a thin, steady note that isn't a whistle so much as a held tone. Somewhere, metal answers—wind chimes, maybe, or something smaller catching rhythm by accident.

A tune moves through it. Not melody exactly. Cadence. The shape of a hymn carried half-remembered, wind taking the words and leaving the bones. DeeDee used to hum like that—never loud, never finishing a line. As if completing it might make it real.

The sound doesn't comfort me.

It steadies something.

Mae exhales across the room. Not a sigh. A release that knows it wasn't earned. My parents' voices soften in the kitchen, dropping into that careful, domestic register people use when they're trying not to disturb something already awake.

Dara doesn't move.

That's when I understand what's been wrong with the way I've been reading the room.

This isn't tension waiting to be resolved. It's history holding itself open, checking whether it's finally being seen accurately. Not asking to be soothed. Not asking to be named. Just refusing to compress itself into something easier to live with.

The Quiet in me settles back—not smoothed down, not dismissed—simply present. Like a hand returning to a table after deciding not to knock.

The house doesn't relax. It **accepts**.

That's different.

Acceptance has boundaries. It means something has been acknowledged and will not be moved for convenience again. The weight under the floorboards stays where it is. The air keeps its density. The sound keeps its thin, persistent shape.

I don't feel afraid.

I feel positioned.

Later, I'll understand what this costs. Tonight, I only know that a kind of return has already happened—and it didn't require anyone to open a door.

The house holds.

And now, so do I.

CHAPTER ELEVEN —THE LISTENING

The house sounds different when no one is talking.

It isn't silent—never that—but the noises thin out, spread farther apart, as if whatever lives in the walls has begun conserving energy. Footsteps land softer. Doors close more carefully. Even breathing seems negotiated.

I notice it first in the way the floor responds. Not creaking exactly. More like testing. A small give under my weight where there hadn't been one earlier, the boards warming just enough to register presence and then cooling again.

Listening.

I move from room to room without purpose, pretending to straighten things that don't need it. A chair nudged back into place. A folded blanket smoothed. Each action feels ceremonial without being chosen as such, like my body remembers how to behave in houses that pay attention.

Outside, the wind shifts direction. It comes from the hill now instead of the lane, carrying the faint scrape of branches rubbing where they shouldn't be able to reach. I pause near the window, watching the glass darken where my reflection overlays the yard.

For a moment, it feels like the land is looking back.

Not at my face. At my outline. At the way I occupy space.

I don't press against it. I've learned better than that. Pressing invites resistance. Instead, I let my weight settle, let my Quiet rest the way a hand does when it's finally accepted a surface.

Somewhere behind me, the house gives a small sound—approval or adjustment, I can't tell. The difference between those two things has always been subtle.

I tell myself it's just age. Old houses make old sounds. Fields shift. Trees rub. None of this needs a name.

But the longer I stand there, the more aware I become of how *exact* the timing is. How each sound arrives only after I stop moving. How the land waits for stillness before answering.

I step back from the window.

Immediately, the sense fades—not gone, just retracted. Like an animal pulling its head back into cover.

That's when I understand what's changed.

The land isn't reacting to us anymore.

It's tracking us.

CHAPTER TWELVE— THE NIGHT WALK

The storm doesn't arrive all at once.

It builds the way trouble does out here—slow, steady, already decided long before anyone looks up to notice.

By late afternoon, the sky has gone the flat, pewter color of old spoons. Wind worries the pine tops in long, low shivers. The local AM station crackles from the small radio on the kitchen counter, the weatherman's voice thin with static.

"Winter system moving in faster than expected… gusts… possible outages…"

My mother turns the volume down but doesn't switch it off. My father watches the window as if the land is about to deliver a verdict.

Dara stands in the doorway between kitchen and living room, shoulder resting lightly against the frame. Her eyes are unfocused, soft in a way that never means gentle, lips curled in a strange delight.

"It's starting," she says.

No one asks what she means.

Weather. Memory. Both.

By the time darkness comes, it feels less like an evening and more like a closing.

We eat early. Stew this time. Bread warmed in the oven. My mother sets the table with the old grace that never left her hands. My father says grace over bowls and steam, voice low, the familiar cadence worn smooth.

"…and forgive us our debts…"

He stumbles there. Just slightly. Then recovers and continues.

Dara's mouth curves. Not quite a smile. Not sympathy either.

After dinner, my mother clears plates as if the approaching storm is simply another chore.

My father disappears down the hallway and returns with the big family Bible—PaPa's Bible—the one that used to live on a special side table in their old living room. Bicentennial Bible with all the Presidents 'pictures and biographies. Proud 1976—the year people replaced light switches with American Eagles. The leather is cracked, slightly greyed where hands held it for years. He sets it gently on the coffee table by the fireplace, as if it's another person taking a seat.

"I thought you left that at the house," Mae says.

He shrugs one shoulder. "I brought it. Thought it ought to see this place again."

I sit on the couch near the corner. Mae takes the floor, back against the side. Dara sits in PaPa's old recliner without asking.

The storm taps at the windows, rain first, then something sharper—ice, or the beginning of snow.

My father opens the Bible.

Loose things live between the pages. Old bulletins. Obituaries. Bookmarks from churches that no longer exist or changed their names to sound less like judgment.

One glossy rectangle slips out and lands on the table—a funeral card. White lilies, script font, the kind DeeDee always ordered in bulk "because it's just better to have them." Her voice comes back to me all English-southern drawn.

Mae reaches for the card. Her fingers stop just short.

"Whose is that?" she asks.

My father clears his throat. "Just let it be."

Dara leans forward, taking it like she has every right.

The name is on her side; I can't see it. But I recognize the style—aged, small-town, with a gold border. DeeDee's taste all over it. Old school simplicity. Nothing like her diamonds.

Dara reads silently, then looks up at my father.

"This was his," she says.

My father's jaw works once. Twice. "It was a long time ago."

"Still his," Dara says.

The storm presses harder at the windows. The house groans, a low, old-man sound.

My mother takes the card from Dara's hand with more force than necessary. She tucks it back into the Bible without marking where it fell from.

My father turns a page at random, landing on a verse already underlined in shaky ink.

"For there is nothing covered, that shall not be revealed; neither hid, that shall not be known." — Luke 12:2

He reads it aloud before he realizes he's done it.

Silence follows.

Thin. Tight.

"That was your grandfather's favorite," my mother says. Her voice has no warmth in it.

Mae looks from the Bible to our father. "Was it?"

He doesn't answer.

Dara watches him. Then us.

Her gaze moves like a finger along a seam.

"He used to say that," she murmurs. "When he took us down to the lake."

My chest pulls tight. "We're not doing this."

Dara's eyes flick to me, quick, pleased. "You remember more than you think, Claire."

The lights flicker once.

Just once.

Long enough for the house to show us what it looks like without them.

Then everything goes dark.

It isn't theatrical dark. No bang. No scream. Just absence.

The heater cuts off mid-breath. The fridge clicks silent. The small, constant hum of the house vanishes, and what's left is the storm and our own breathing.

The air pricks along my arms—charged, waiting. The old Quiet in me lifts its head, wanting to smooth everything down, to press the edges flat.

My mother prays softly under her breath—just a few indiscernible words, the ones she used to say in times of stress.

My father closes the Bible like that can keep anything in.

"We'll need light if this keeps up," he says. "And something for backup heat."

"I'll go," I say automatically.

Mae is already standing. "We'll both go."

My mother clicks on her phone flashlight, the thin white beam making the room strange. She hands it to me, then takes a candle from the mantle and begins digging through a drawer for matches.

Her movements are brisk. Controlled. The way you hold back panic when there are still other people in the room.

"Don't we have anything else if the power stays off?" I ask.

She exhales once, short. "The listing said… hang on." She wipes her hands, pulls her reading glasses from her pocket, and taps at her phone.

A message thread glows faint blue in the dark—a cheerful profile picture I remember from when I booked the place. Smiling couple. Flannel. Teeth a little too white for farm people. His eyes catch the camera flash wrong—too bright, like the light bounced off instead of into them.

So glad you're staying with us! If there's a storm, don't worry—there are emergency supplies in the small outbuilding by the gravel road. Little gray shed. Kerosene lamps, extra fuel, and a small generator if you need it. We'll check on things when roads are clear 👍

My stomach sinks. "The outbuilding. Outside."

"In this?" Mae says.

A gust hits the side of the house hard enough to rattle the windows. Something—ice, snow, both—scrapes along the siding.

"We'll be fine," I say, more for my mother than for myself. "It's not far."

My father sits very still, hands folded over the closed Bible. In the candle's early light, his face looks older than it did this morning. Or maybe just truer.

For a moment, the flame bends, and the room shifts with it.

In the front window glass, a reflection flashes—too tall, too still—and for half a second it looks like the man from the listing photo. His eyes catch the light wrong there too, brightening instead of dimming, like the shine comes from behind them, not off them.

I don't breathe.

The air around me tightens, edges humming as if something in the room recognizes him before I do. I smooth the feeling down—quieting it—out of instinct more than intent.

"I'll come," he says.

"You will not," my mother snaps. "You'll fall on that ice and then we'll really be in trouble."

Her fear shows itself in bossiness. It always has. Scotch-Irish strength.

Mae pulls her coat from the hook. I do the same.

Dara doesn't move.

Then she does.

"I'll go with you," she says.

My first instinct is no. It comes up fast, cold, from somewhere lower than my lungs.

"I don't think—" I start.

"She's right to come," my father interrupts. His voice is flat. Resigned more than firm. "No one goes out alone."

He may mean us. He may mean something else.

My mother thrusts another candle into Dara's hand, then changes her mind, swaps it for a flashlight from the junk drawer.

"Don't wander," she says. "You go to the shed, you grab what you need, and you come right back."

DeeDee echoes in my memory, Southeastern Missouri vowels and Sunday perfume:

Now don't wander, this land doesn't forget a thing.

My hand finds the doorknob. Cold leaks through the metal.

I open it.

The night hits us like a wall.

The storm hasn't landed fully yet, but it's close.

Snow comes in hard, slanting sheets, more ice than powder. The wind shoves at us sideways, mean and insistent. The porch light is out now, but our flashlights carve narrow tunnels through the dark.

The world beyond the beam feels huge and empty and too close all at once.

We step down carefully. Boards slick. Gravel hidden under a thin layer of refreezing slush. The gray shed waits at the edge of the lane, small and square against the field's emptiness.

Behind it, farther up the slope, the graveyard hill is just a darker shadow against the sky. I can't see the stones from here, but I know exactly where his is. Third from the right. Slanted. A name we still don't say aloud.

The wind carries the faint clang of the graveyard gate knocking itself open and shut.

We walk.

No one talks.

The snow does enough speaking—hitting our coats, our faces, the ground. My flashlight bounces over the path, catching the ghost shapes of fence posts, the glint of ice on low branches.

"Wonder Bread bags would come in handy," Mae mutters.

The line makes something in my chest loosen. "Mom would've doubled them up for this."

Dara walks half a step behind us. Her flashlight stays low, steady, not swinging at all—as if she already knows where everything is.

We reach the halfway point between the house and the shed.

That's when I see the footprints.

They're not ours—too many, too layered. The snow hasn't had time to cover them yet. They lead from the direction of the lane toward the house.

A mix of sizes.

Boot treads. Heavy, adult, edges clean.

And smaller ones.

Not child-small. Just… narrow. Light.

Impressions that don't bite deep into the snow the first time, but leave a second shadow when someone is dragged back over them.

Something presses at my ears then—a low density shift, like the air is thinking about what it wants. The Quiet in me notices before I do, bracing, ready to push back.

I stop. Mae nearly collides with me. "What—"

I angle the beam down. She sees them too.

"Maybe the owners came by earlier," she says quickly. "Before the storm."

"In this?" I ask.

The lane is empty. No fresh tire tracks. Nothing but the wide, pale sheet of field and the black shape of the road beyond.

"They said they'd come when the roads were clear," Mae adds, quieter. "Not... not during."

Dara steps around us, following the footprints with her light. Her hair whips across her face in the wind but she doesn't brush it away.

"They were here," she says, almost serene. "They always come back to check."

"Check what?" I ask.

She doesn't answer.

The shed looms closer now—tin roof, gray siding, a small cross hammered crooked above the door. A plain wooden cross like the old country churches used to hang.

Even in the storm, it catches the light just right, in the crystallizing snowflakes—rhinestones sprinkled into metal, making it glitter like something DeeDee would've worn on a chain over her polyester Sunday pantsuit.

My throat goes dry.

Mae sees it too. "Oh my lands."

"It looks like her," I say.

We don't have to say who.

DeeDee, with her "diamond" crosses and her know-it-all talking, and her way of turning other people's comments into a humbling humiliation. PaPa's arm always offered for her to lean on, supporting all of her behavior—good and poor.

Dara reaches up and touches the cross lightly, her gloved finger tracing one edge.

"She bought this," she says. "Said the place needed blessings."

The wind gusts hard enough to rock me on my feet. Somewhere up on the graveyard hill, something metallic slams and drags. Gate. Sign. Both.

"We're getting what we need," I say. "That's it."

I pull the shed door. It sticks once, then gives.

Inside, the air is colder than outside—a cold that feels like it's coming from the walls instead of the weather.

Our lights pick up the shine off metal—tools hanging in careful rows, a red gas can, stacks of feed that no one has bothered to cover.

On a low shelf, three kerosene lamps sit in a neat line, glass cloudy, wicks trimmed like someone checked them not that long ago.

Beside them: a cracked plastic tub of matches, a coil of extension cord, two more gas cans pushed back into the shadows.

There's an empty rectangle on the floor where something big used to sit. The concrete is cleaner there, dust scuffed in a wide arc like it was dragged instead of lifted.

"The generator," Mae says quietly.

"It was supposed to be here," I answer.

My light follows the drag marks toward the door and loses them in the churned snow just outside the threshold.

Behind us, the wind stops for one strange second— like it's listening.

The quiet shifts from ordinary to intentional. The Quiet inside me feels it too, that tilt toward attention, and rises like a hand between us and whatever is looking.

Then, from somewhere closer to the graveyard than to the lane, we hear it.

A long, low creak of metal.

The sound a gate makes when it's being pushed slowly open by a hand, not the wind.

My heart knocks once, hard.

"We're going back," I say. "Now."

Dara doesn't move immediately. Her flashlight has drifted toward the fields, the beam catching nothing but snow and dark.

"He doesn't like the lights on," she says softly.

For a heartbeat, I don't know if she means the boy— or someone else. PaPa. The owners. All that is holy.

"Then he's out of luck," I say.

I set one of the lamps down harder than I mean to. The glass rattles in the small space, too loud.

Then we're back outside, pulling the shed door shut, heading toward the house.

The footprints are harder to see now, partly filled by new snow, partly smeared by our own.

The lights are still out at the house. No welcoming glow. No porch lamp.

Just the shape of it against the storm, low and long and waiting.

Halfway back, Mae leans close.

"Look," she whispers.

Her beam swings toward the graveyard hill.

Snow and dark. The faint lift of stones.

For a second, I think that's all.

Then lightning flares—thin but bright, spiderwebbing behind the clouds—and the hill snaps into stark white.

Fence. Leaning stones.

And a figure.

Not close enough to make out a face. Just a blacker shadow against the dark, near where we stood the day we visited the graves.

Near that third stone from the right.

Something in the air presses in, a soft weight inside my ears. The Quiet in me answers on instinct, smoothing down, as if I can press the moment flat before it notices us.

By the time my eyes adjust, the lightning is gone. The hill is just a hill again.

"Did you—" Mae starts.

"Yes," I say.

We don't say what we saw.

Or who.

We hurry the rest of the way.

Inside, the house is dim—just candles now, small islands of gold on the coffee table, the counter, the hallway table that used to hold framed pictures of us as kids.

My mother meets us at the door, eyes wide, hands tight on the dish towel she's forgotten to set down.

"Well?" she sweetly demands.

"There are lamps and fuel," I say. "But the generator that was supposed to be there is gone."

My father sits in his chair with the Bible closed on his lap, fingers resting on the cover as if he's holding it in place. The shadows carve his face into someone older.

Or more honest.

"So we're on candles and whatever heat we've got left," my mother says. "Storm or not."

"Looks that way," I say.

I don't believe it's only the storm.

Dara closes the door gently behind us, turning the lock with a quiet, decisive click.

"Feels better in the dark anyway," she says.

None of us answer.

The house breathes around us—wood settling, wind pushing, something small moving in the walls. The storm throws handfuls of ice against the windows.

In the candlelight, the family Bible looks larger than it did earlier.

A weight on the table. A witness.

My father clears his throat. "We'll stay in the main room tonight," he says. "All of us. Bring your blankets. No one wanders."

For once, there is no other suggestion from my mother.

We gather our blankets. For a while, we do as we're told.

Obedience frays faster in this house.

Mae meets my eyes.

Dara watches us both, her expression unreadable, her body held at an angle that could be protection—or aim.

Outside, the storm gathers itself.

Inside, the dark deepens.

It doesn't feel like we lost the lights.

It feels like something turned them off.

CHAPTER THIRTEEN— THE WITNESS

We take our glasses to the back bedroom like teenagers trying not to wake the house—poured earlier in the kitchen, nothing fancy, just something to hold.

Mae closes the door with care—slow turn of the knob, latch eased into place—then leans her shoulder against it for a second longer than necessary. I set the glasses on the dresser instead of the nightstand. The wood is scarred there, old dents from moves and reuses, from being dragged instead of lifted.

The lamp stays off. We use our phones for light, tilted low so it doesn't leak under the door.

"Just a quick one," Mae says, already sitting on the edge of the bed. Her voice is brighter than it's been all night. "We just need a minute."

I don't argue. I hand her the glass. The smell of alcohol is sharp in the small space. We drink carefully, like we're afraid of spilling more than liquid.

Outside, the storm presses at the house, but it's muted back here. Distant. Contained.

For a moment, it almost works.

Mae exhales, shoulders dropping. "Geez," she says. "I forgot how cold it gets in these places. It's like the land refuses to warm up for strangers."

I nod. I'm watching the shadow of the window frame tremble on the wall. The Quiet in me is still—present, but not interfering. Just holding.

"We got back," Mae says, as if she needs to hear it said. "That's what matters."

"Yes," I say. Not because it's true. Because it's the sentence she needs.

She takes another sip. "Do you think Dad's asleep?"

"I don't know."

Mae's mouth twists. "He shouldn't have come. This was a bad idea."

"It's already happened," I say, gently. "Let's not redo it tonight."

She gives a weak laugh. "That's rich, coming from you."

I'm about to answer when the door opens.

No knock. Just the quiet click of the latch turning, the door easing inward like it's always belonged to her.

Dara steps inside and closes it behind her.

She notices the glasses immediately. Her eyes flick from one to the other. Her smile is small—not amused. Interested.

"So this is where you went," she says. "I wondered."

Mae sits up straighter. "We needed a minute."

Dara hums softly, as if considering whether that's true. "You always did."

"This isn't a group thing," Mae says.

Dara's gaze slides to me. "Isn't it?"

The room feels smaller with her in it. The air thickens—not threatening. Intentional.

"Go back out," Mae says, too quickly. "Mom will—"

"Mom's busy worrying about Dad," Dara says. "Dad's busy pretending he didn't see what he saw."

She takes the empty spot at the foot of the bed without asking. Not sitting fully. Perching. Ready to move or strike.

"And you two," she continues, "are hiding in here drinking like that makes tonight something else."

Mae's face flushes. "Stop."

Dara tilts her head. "Stop what?"

"This." Mae gestures helplessly. "This thing you're doing."

Dara's eyes brighten. "Talking?"

Mae's breath stutters. She looks at me. "Say something."

The Quiet stirs—an old, familiar readiness. I could smooth this. I could press Dara back into silence, let the room go soft around the edges.

I don't.

"You don't have to do this," I say instead.

Dara smiles at that. "I absolutely do."

She reaches out and takes Mae's glass, lifting it just enough to inspect the line of liquid left inside. "Brave choice," she says. "Keeping it tidy."

Mae snatches the glass back. "You don't get to judge or insert yourself."

"I'm not," Dara says. "I'm observing."

That word lands wrong. Heavy.

"You saw it," Dara says, casual. "Up there."

Mae's jaw tightens. "We're not—"

"Going to talk about it?" Dara finishes. "Of course not."

I feel the Quiet steady, the way it does when something irreversible is approaching.

Mae's voice lowers. "It was the storm. Lightning. Shadows."

Dara nods as if agreeing. "That's one explanation."

Mae grips the blanket beside her. "That's the explanation."

Dara's gaze doesn't leave her face. "Then say it was an accident."

Silence stretches taut.

Mae swallows. Her throat works. "It was—"

Nothing comes out.

Dara's smile grows sharper. "See? If it was an accident, that should've been easy."

Mae's eyes shine, furious and wet. "You're cruel."

Dara considers that. "No. I'm honest."

The Quiet flares—hot, immediate. The instinct to stop this presses hard against my ribs.

And with it comes recognition.

Stopping her would erase what Mae is feeling right now. The truth clawing its way forward, the cost of not saying it already bruising.

"This isn't fair," Mae says, voice breaking. "You don't get to do this to us."

Dara's voice softens. "Us?"

Mae stares at her. "You weren't even there."

Dara nods. "Not then. But I knew. I always knew."

That certainty is worse than a confession.

I step forward, not toward Dara, but between them. Not blocking. Grounding.

"You're not allowed to turn this into a performance," I say. "If you're going to say it, you own the weight."

Dara's eyes flicker—annoyance, then interest.

"I do," she says. "That's the difference between us."

Mae shakes her head violently. "No. You looked away too."

Dara smiles. "Looking away isn't the same as not knowing."

The room feels pinned then—like the walls have leaned in just enough to listen.

I feel the Quiet move—not outward, not forceful. It doesn't hush Dara. It doesn't rescue Mae.

It **anchors** the moment.

"No more erasing," I say. "Not tonight. Not again."

Dara studies me, calculating. Then she sits fully on the bed, settling her weight like she plans to stay.

"Good," she says. "That's all I wanted."

Mae's face crumples, not in tears—something older. Defeated. Seen.

The truth doesn't explode. It doesn't need to.

It occupies the room the way something heavy does when you finally stop pretending it isn't there.

Outside, the storm rakes the house.

Inside, the bedroom holds.

Three sisters. One memory. No way out that doesn't cost something.

And for the first time, the cost belongs to all of us.

CHAPTER FOURTEEN—THE KEEPING

At night, the land forgets nothing.

It loosens during the day—lets sunlight wash over it, lets birds and wind rearrange the story into something easier to carry. But darkness tightens the weave. Pulls old threads to the surface.

I sit without reason and know immediately where I am.

The house is still. The storm has moved on, leaving behind a cold that doesn't come from the weather. Somewhere, a drip repeats itself, slow and deliberate, marking time the way it always has here.

I don't check my phone for the time. Time behaves differently in places like this.

Instead, I still and listen.

Not for footsteps. Not for voices.

For *placement*.

Something in the land has shifted its attention uphill. Toward the graves. Toward the slope where names tilt and sink and wait. I feel it the way you feel a change in pressure before a headache—dull, insistent, unavoidable.

I don't look.

I've learned the cost of looking.

The Quiet stirs but doesn't rise. It understands this moment doesn't require interference. Observation is enough. Bearing witness without response.

The house creaks once, softly, like a warning meant only for itself.

Then comes the sound I've been expecting.

Not a step.

A *transfer*.

Weight moving from one place to another where weight shouldn't be. The unmistakable sense of something being set down carefully, with intent.

My breath holds. Not out of fear. Out of recognition.

The land has decided something.

Not about us.

About *sequence*.

I don't know yet what comes next. Only that whatever happened before has been acknowledged, recorded, and filed somewhere deeper than memory. Not forgiven. Not punished.

Kept.

When sleep finally returns, it will so without images. Just pressure. Just depth.

Morning will not erase this.

Nothing does.

No one says goodnight.

We scatter the way people do when they don't want to risk another sentence—separate rooms, separate breaths, each of us pretending there's something practical to be done that requires distance.

Mae takes the couch. I hear her shake the blanket once, too hard, then go still. My parents move down the hall together without touching. A door closes. Another follows. Dara goes somewhere I don't track. I don't need to.

I stay where I am longer than necessary, standing in the dim of the living room, listening to the house relearn us.

The storm has eased into something steadier. Less dramatic. More committed. Ice ticks against the windows in a patient rhythm. The wind doesn't gust anymore; it leans. The house answers with small creaks, joints settling, the sound of weight redistributed.

The Bible is still on the coffee table.

I consider moving it. Just shifting it to the shelf. Tidying up the room so it doesn't look like something happened here.

I don't.

Instead, I turn off one kerosene lamp, then another, until only a single candle remains, guttering low. The shadow the Bible throws stretches longer than it should. I leave it that way.

Sleep doesn't take me cleanly.

When it comes, it does so in patches—short, shallow intervals where my body rests but my mind stays alert, listening. I drift off and surface again to the sounds of the house: a pipe knocking once, footsteps that aren't footsteps, the wind searching for places it hasn't tried yet.

At one point, I wake convinced I heard my name. At another, I'm sure someone is standing just outside the doorway, waiting for me to notice.

Nothing is there.

Morning arrives without ceremony.

The light is wrong—flat, bleached, filtered through cloud and ice. It doesn't warm anything it touches. The power is still out. The house holds its breath.

I make coffee from habit, then realize there's no electricity and stand there longer than I need to, holding the kettle like it might solve something if I wait. I set the kettle down and light the small burner on the stove—the old manual one my parents insisted on keeping years ago "just in case." The flame catches unevenly, blue licking low and stubborn beneath the metal. I fill the kettle from the tap, cold water biting my fingers, and set it back over the heat. It takes longer this way. The sound is different too—no familiar hum, just the soft, patient tick of warming metal. I stay there until steam begins to whisper at the spout, until the ordinary act feels earned again.

When I finally heat water another way, the smell grounds me. Bitter. Familiar. My hands shake just enough to notice.

Mae emerges wrapped in the blanket from the couch, hair pulled back with no care taken. Her eyes meet mine once, then slide away. She doesn't speak.

"You sleep?" I ask.

She shrugs. "Enough."

We exist in parallel for a while—me at the counter, her at the window, both of us careful not to touch the space where last night still hums.

My parents appear eventually. Quiet. Polite. My mother asks about the storm. My father answers with facts pulled from the radio reports of his childhood, things remembered because they're safer than the present.

No one mentions Dara.

She's not gone. I can feel that. Her absence has a shape. It sits somewhere on the house like a weight you don't see but compensate for anyway.

Somewhere outside, the wind finds the chimes again—the old ones hung near the back of the house, thin metal tubes knocking together out of rhythm. The sound drifts in through the walls, uneven, half-familiar. Not music exactly. More like memory testing itself, seeing what still answers.

The Quiet in me is subdued—not pressed down, not stirred. It feels like something after exertion. A muscle waiting to see what it will be asked to do next.

The melody comes without invitation. No words at first—just the lift and fall, the shape of it carried on DeeDee's breath years ago, humming while she folded towels or stirred something on the stove. Then the line settles in, clear as if spoken beside my ear: *And He walks with me, and He talks with me.* It doesn't comfort. It doesn't accuse. It simply arrives, the way old things do when the house goes quiet enough to remember itself.

I step outside alone.

The air is sharp, clean, unforgiving. Snow has crusted into ice where it fell. The path to the shed is half-erased, our footprints softened but not gone. The graveyard hill is still there, of course—unbothered, unimpressed, its stones keeping their own counsel.

I don't climb it.

I don't need to.

The knowledge isn't located there anymore. It's inside the house now, threaded through rooms and routines, settled into corners.

Behind me, the house creaks—not a warning, not an invitation. Recognition.

And He tells me I am His own. The words run their course whether I agree with them or not. *For the love we share as we tarry there...* I don't finish it. I never do. The rest dissolves into wind and chimes and cold air, into the weight of standing still when movement would feel like pretending.

I stand there until the cold burns, until my breath fogs thick enough to obscure the view, until I'm certain that what happened last night didn't disappear just because daylight showed up without asking permission.

When I go back inside, Mae is sitting at the table with a mug she hasn't touched. She looks smaller in daylight. Or maybe just more exposed.

"You didn't stop her," she says, without accusation.

"No," I answer.

She nods. Once. Acceptance without forgiveness.

"That matters," she says. She doesn't specify how. She doesn't need to.

Later, things will have to be decided. Conversations will be had. Lines will be drawn and redrawn.

Not today.

Today is for containment.

The house understands that.

It keeps us close. It keeps the noise low. It holds the truth exactly where it landed and doesn't ask us to do anything with it yet.

That restraint—earned, not enforced—feels like the only mercy we're allowed.

The chimes sound once more, softer this time, as if the wind has learned where to touch them without making a demand. The song fades with them—not gone, just set aside—waiting for another quiet, another night, another moment when no one is speaking and the house decides to fill the space itself.

CHAPTER SIXTEEN — WHAT HOLDS

The house stays quiet after the night finishes breaking over us.

Not the hush of sleep. Something more deliberate. As if everything that needed saying has already been said and the walls are waiting to see whether we'll respect that.

I wake before anyone else. The storm has thinned but not cleared. Wind slides along the siding, cautious now, testing what's left. Snow taps the windows in small, patient shifts.

In the bathroom, I turn on the tap. The pipes answer slowly. When the heat comes, it arrives uneven—lukewarm first, then hotter than expected, steam lifting against the mirror.

I hold my hands under it longer than necessary. The heat blooms slowly, rising into my wrists, my forearms, the small bones that always ache first in winter. I let the sensation register fully—the sting, then the soft surrender. Water knows how to wait. It doesn't insist on change. It adjusts, minute by minute, until the body remembers how to receive it. I watch the steam fog the mirror, then fade, then gather again. The shape of my face appears and disappears in fragments—eye, mouth, cheekbone—never all at once. That feels right too. Wholeness is overrated when you're trying to remain intact.

The hymn returns in pieces, not melody, just cadence. The remembered sway of voices in a room with bad acoustics. Someone a half-beat off. Someone else too loud.

The comfort wasn't in the words. It was in the repetition. Knowing what came next without needing to think.

I dry my hands carefully. Turn the faucet all the way off. Make sure it's done.

Not to clean them. To feel weight.

Water has always been good for that—pressure without argument, warmth that asks nothing in return. My fingers loosen. The Quiet settles into the shape of my palms, not expanding, not retreating. Just present. Holding.

A line from DeeDee's hymn drifts up without warning. Fragmented. Uninvited.

And He walks with me…

I don't finish it. I don't need to. The words don't want to be sung; they want to be remembered as sound—half-heard, carried through rooms where someone else believed them more fully than I ever did.

I shut off the tap. Dry my hands. Leave the bathroom dark.

The house does not react.

That feels important.

I pull on boots and a coat and step out onto the back porch without waking anyone. The door closes softly behind me, the latch clicking into place with care. The storm breathes across the yard, cold and awake. The porch boards creak once under my weight, then settle. I pause there, long enough to feel the difference between the cold outside and the warmth pressing faintly at my back. The house doesn't pull me in. It doesn't urge me out. It allows the distance.

Snow clings to the railing in thin seams, packed by the wind into corners where a hand might rest. I think about how many times mine did. How often I leaned there without noticing what I was asking the land to hold.

The Quiet aligns itself—not forward, not outward. It stays vertical, like a spine remembering its job.

The land opens in familiar sections—paths worn thin by work, not wandering. This isn't the part people tell stories about. This is the part that kept everyone fed.

I take the slope down toward where the pig pens used to sit. The fence is mostly gone now—posts still standing in uneven patience, wire sagging where it hasn't been claimed by rust or grass. The ground here is packed hard, soil dark and dense even under snow. Years of weight pressed into it.

Animals teach land how to hold. This ground took weight daily, predictably. It learned the rhythm of hunger and release, of noise at feeding time and the sudden, almost offended quiet afterward. The land here wasn't asked to remember grief. It was asked to support continuity. There's dignity in that kind of labor.

I press the sole of my boot down and feel how little it gives. Even now, even after years of neglect, the earth remembers what it was shaped for.

That memory is steadier than fear.

I stop where the trough once stood. I can still see it— the way the mud pooled there no matter how carefully it was drained, the way PaPa used to knock ice loose with the heel of his boot, cussing quietly, practical devotion in every motion.

The Quiet presses lightly then. Not warning. Just acknowledgment.

Work leaves different traces than harm. This place knows the difference.

I follow the edge of the property toward the old slaughter shed. It's barely standing—roof sagged inward, boards split, the door hanging crooked on one hinge. DeeDee never liked this spot. Said it felt "heavy." PaPa told her heavy wasn't the same as bad.

Inside, the air smells like iron memory and old sawdust. Not blood. That faded long ago. What's left is the echo of purpose—quick, necessary, not unkind. Death that fed people. Endings with reason.

I don't go in. There are places where the past doesn't want revisiting—only acknowledgment. PaPa understood that. He knew the difference between honoring a thing and reopening it. The shed doesn't ask me to bear witness again. It knows what it was used for. That was enough.

The Quiet hums once, low and satisfied, then stills.

I don't need to.

The land isn't asking me to witness anything new.

Beyond that, the slope steepens toward the bottom of the hill, where the old cabin still hunkers between trees. Not the haunted house. Never that. This one was used. Someone lived there once. Ate there. Slept through storms like this and woke up to do it again.

The path down is slick. Snow hides the rocks PaPa warned us about with the same words every time. *Watch your footing. Land 'll turn on you if you get careless.* I remember his voice more clearly than his face in moments like this. Instruction without softness, without apology. Love that assumed competence. Love that trusted the body to learn.

I move slower because of it. Not afraid. Just attentive.

I take my time.

The cabin sits low and unremarkable, roofline barely visible under white. No drama to it. No invitation. Just presence. I stand outside and let the wind move around me, feeling how far the Quiet goes.

It doesn't reach.

Or rather—it does, but it stays contained within me. The land doesn't accept it, doesn't resist it. There's a difference. This place is complete without my attention. It has its own boundaries, earned long before I learned how to feel them.

That realization lands heavier than anything else has.

I don't belong to this land the way I thought I did.

And it doesn't belong to me.

That mutual independence feels like relief.

On the way back up the hill, snow shifts under my boots, the wind rising just enough to remind me where the edges are. The storm doesn't welcome me; it tolerates me. I respect that.

Halfway back, I stop and turn.

The house waits at the top of the rise—not looming, not inviting. Neutral. Its windows dark. Its roofline steady against the moving sky. It looks like a place that knows how to keep what's put inside it, nothing more.

That, too, feels right. Right doesn't mean easy. It means aligned. The kind of right that doesn't argue with you afterward, that doesn't echo. It simply holds its shape and waits to see whether you will respect it.

My breath steadies as I turn back toward the house. Not relief—clarity. The difference matters.

By the time I step onto the porch again, the cold has worked its way deep into my bones. Not painful. Just present.

The door opens easily. Warmth meets me in a measured wave.

Inside, the house is quiet in a new way—not braced, not listening hard. Holding, but not tightly.

Everyone else is still asleep.

I hang my coat. Sit at the table. Let my hands rest flat against the wood. The Quiet smooths itself down without instruction, not retreating, not searching.

This isn't resolution. It isn't victory. It's alignment.

Whatever happened here remains. Whatever was set in motion hasn't finished moving. Dara's shape still presses at the edge of things—not here, not now, but not gone either.

And still—the land holds.

Not to protect us. Not to forgive. Just to remain itself.

I can work with that.

When the house stirs and the day finally begins, nothing feels lighter. But nothing feels unstable either.

That's enough.

For now.

CHAPTER SEVENTEEN—THE LINE

Later, with the house awake around me, I take my coffee outside. I follow the edge again, letting the cold decide how much of me it gets.

By daylight, the land pretends to be neutral again.

Snow crusts the field into something almost harmless. Fences stand where fences should. Even the hill looks ordinary from a distance, softened by light and familiarity.

Up close, it's different.

I stop at the edge of where the ground begins to rise, toe nudging into frozen soil. The line is subtle—no fence, no marker—but my body knows where not to go.

The Quiet reacts the same way. Not alarmed. Restrained.

This isn't fear territory.

This is boundary.

I think of the way animals move around places like this. The invisible arcs they trace instinctively, honoring lines no one taught them to see. Old agreements carried forward without question.

The wind cuts across my face, sharper here, as if the land resents proximity without purpose. The message is clear enough.

You can stand. You can look. You cannot cross.

I step back, and the pressure eases immediately—not relieved, but satisfied.

That's the difference.

Satisfaction feels older than mercy.

Behind me, the house waits, patient and unmistakably aligned with the land's decision. Whatever happens next will happen inside those boundaries. Whatever escapes them will not come back unchanged.

I don't challenge it.

Some understandings are not meant to be tested.

The day doesn't end. It just loses its edges.

Afternoon slips sideways instead of forward, the light thinning without fully dimming, as if the sky can't decide what to do with what's already happened. No one suggests dinner. No one checks the time. Hunger exists, but it doesn't assert itself.

The house stays unchanged. That's the difference.

Not attentive. Not braced. Just quiet in a way that implies patience.

Mae sits at the table with her hands folded, her elbows carefully placed so they don't cross the faint ring left by an old mug. She doesn't look up when I enter the room. She already knows where I am. We've been tracking each other without trying.

My mother moves from room to room and back again, adjusting things that don't need adjusting. A curtain smoothed. A chair aligned with the table. It isn't nervousness. It's maintenance — the what that you do when you need your surroundings to reflect order, even if nothing else will.

My father stands near the back door, staring at the glass. The storm has thinned to gray movement and sound, rain scraping intermittently at the siding like a reminder that weather continues even when people stall.

No one speaks.

There are things that could be said. I feel them assemble and disband inside my chest like pieces that don't want to lock together yet.

The line holds because I let it.

That turns out to be harder now than when I drew it.

I cross into the living room and sit in a chair that doesn't belong to anyone in particular. The cushions dip slightly, familiar and unforgiving. Across from me, the chair Dara chose last night remains empty. Someone pushed it back under the table at some point. Not conspicuously. Just enough that it no longer invites.

The absence doesn't feel safer.

It feels accounted for.

A floorboard ticks once. The sound moves through the room and stops. No one reacts. The house has done this before. It will do it again. Today just happens to be louder on the inside.

Mae finally exhales, long and measured. She looks at me then, her expression guarded but steady.

"Did we—do something?" she starts.

I shake my head once.

She nods and doesn't try again.

That restraint travels through the room, subtle but real. It reaches my father, whose shoulders settle by a degree. My mother pauses in the doorway, hands empty now, and lets them stay that way.

Holding doesn't ease the weight. It redistributes it.

The land outside remains exactly where it was this morning. The slope beyond the house. The tree line. The darker cut where the path disappears downward. Nothing announces itself. Nothing asks to be named.

That's how I know we haven't been forgiven.

We've just been allowed to remain.

Time advances only because it must. The light dulls further. The interior of the house gathers itself inward, not closing — consolidating.

I don't reach for the Quiet. It's there, steady and contained, like a muscle held at readiness but not engaged. I understand now that using it here would be a mistake. The line doesn't need reinforcement. It needs respect.

So I sit.

We all do.

And what's most unsettling isn't that something is waiting.

It's that nothing is.

We are still here.

And the day goes on.

CHAPTER NINETEEN-THE ROOM WHERE WE
WAIT

The candles make the living room look smaller.

Shadows climb the walls in long, reaching shapes, and every familiar piece of furniture becomes a stranger. My father drags the recliner closer to the fireplace, the Bible still in his hands, as if proximity alone might warm him.

My mother lays out quilts with the tense, clipped movements she uses when she's trying not to cry.

"Everyone stays where we can see each other," she keeps saying, though no one has argued. "No wandering tonight. None."

Mae catches my eye over the edge of a folded blanket. Her eyebrows lift—just slightly. *We need a drink.* I nod as the storm hurls itself at the windows in sudden fits, ice smacking the glass in sharp, mean bursts. Somewhere in the back of the house, something knocks once, like a cupboard door settling.

Except this house isn't ours. It has nothing familiar enough to settle.

"I'm going to the kitchen," I tell Mom. "We're grabbing… something."

"What something?" she snaps, too quickly, desperation sharpening the question.

"Calm," Mae answers, already moving.

We cross into the kitchen, our flashlights throwing pale slashes across the cabinets and tile. The candles in the

87

other room leave this space almost completely dark. The air feels colder here, sharper in the corners without the heater's hum. A welcome basket sits on the counter: hot cocoa packets, instant cider, a bottle of cheap Missouri red.

"Red or… red?" I ask.

Mae ignores it and checks the cabinet above the fridge. "There."

A bottle of whiskey. Local. Unlabeled except for a strip of masking tape: 2017.

My stomach dips. "Why would they leave that for guests?"

"They wouldn't," Mae says softly. "This is owner stuff."

We don't say the footprints. We don't say the figure on the hill. We don't say the shed. I take two mugs from the shelf and pour a finger into each. The smell hits—corn mash and a faint hint of apple beneath it.

Mae clinks her mug against mine, humorless. "To Mom not unraveling."

"To Dad not confessing anything terrifying," I say.

"To Dara not murdering us," she finishes.

The whiskey burns clean, a reminder that we're still here, still in our bodies.

A sound interrupts it—a soft scrape, right outside the kitchen door. Mae freezes mid-swallow.

"Tell me that was a branch."

"There aren't trees close enough," I whisper.

We edge toward the window over the sink. The glass is fogged, but I wipe it with my sleeve. Our flashlights reach only the porch steps, the first scatter of gravel, and wind-driven snow. Nothing moves.

But the feeling does.

Something close. Something aware.

Mae swallows. "We're not telling Mom about that."

"Not yet."

"We should go back in."

"Yeah."

We refill our mugs—two fingers this time.

Back in the living room, the air feels tighter, like the house exhaled while we were gone. Mom takes the mug from my hand without looking up, ignoring the smell of whiskey. Dad hasn't moved, except for his thumb tracing a worn crack in the Bible's leather, back and forth like a worry stone.

Dara sits cross-legged near the fireplace, her back to the flames, her face lit only by candles. The glow makes her pupils huge—blacker swallowing black. She looks up when we enter.

"Someone was on the porch," she says calmly.

My skin prickles. "Why do you say that?"

She lifts a small, wet clump of snow from beside her. "Because they brought this in on their boots."

She lets it fall. The melting snow hisses faintly against the warm stone.

Mae tightens her grip on her mug. "Could've been us."

Dara shakes her head. "Yours was slush. This is fresh."

My mother stiffens. "If someone was on the porch—"

"They're not now," Dara says.

Not reassurance. Just a fact.

The storm claws at the house again, louder—like fingernails dragged over siding.

Dad exhales slowly, deliberate. "We'll stay awake in shifts. Three people at all times."

Mom nods, clutching her tea. "I'll take first."

"I will too," Mae says immediately.

Dara's eyes slide to me.

"I'll stay up," I say.

She smiles—not warm, not unkind. The smile of someone who knows a truth before she speaks it.

"Good," she murmurs. "He doesn't like it when the women sleep first."

The room goes very still.

No one asks who he is.

The storm roars as if answering for her.

A dull knock interrupts the quiet—not on the door, but on the far side of the house. A single, heavy thud against the wall. Too low for ice. Too deliberate for wind.

Mom presses a hand to her mouth. Mae jerks closer to me. Dad stands, poker in hand—instinct more than protection. Dara's gaze shifts toward the hallway.

The sound comes again—a scrape, the drag of something along the siding.

"He's circling," Mae whispers.

No one argues.

The noise moves toward the back of the house.

Dad swallows. "That room…"

He stops, breath thinning. "That was my room."

Mom looks at him, confused and afraid—because she doesn't know what he knows.

Dara closes her eyes. "He always went to that window."

Dad's whole face tightens—guilt, memory, something ancient rising through him.

"Don't," he snaps. "Not now. Not tonight."

But the tapping begins.

tap... tap tap

Under the back bedroom window.

Dad lowers his head like the sound touches a place he thought he buried. He whispers something I can't catch. The tapping answers him.

The hallway candle bows sideways, flame nearly horizontal. The air thickens—pressure building, the Quiet in me lifting like it recognizes something older than us.

Then—

a soft rattle against the window glass.

Not storm. Fingers. Testing the latch.

Mom cries out. Dad raises the poker. Mae grips my hand, nails sharp through fabric.

Dara's voice barely stirs the air. "He remembers this house."

The storm shrieks. The window rattles harder.

The rattling stops so suddenly it feels surgical.

Silence pours in—cold, sharp, expectant.

Dad's shoulders remain rigid, poker lifted in a shaking fist. He stares down the dark hallway like he's waiting for a ghost he already knows. Mae leans into me, whispering without sound. Mom clutches the couch, knuckles white, eyes fixed on the flames.

Dara steps back into the candlelight—not closer to us, but no longer facing the hallway.

"He moved," she murmurs.

A soft creak comes from the far left side of the house. A different window.

Closer.

Dad forces the words out. "He can't get in."

It sounds like something he told himself for decades.

Dara tilts her head. "He doesn't want in yet."

My stomach knots. "Then what does he want?"

She looks at me with quiet pity. "To be acknowledged."

Another creak. Closer.

Mom's voice breaks. "We shouldn't have come here. We never should have—"

Dad cuts her off. "Stop. None of this is you."

But he won't look at her. Or at us. His gaze is locked on the floor, jaw tight, as if the truth is pooling there.

"Dad…" Mae whispers. "What was in that room?"

Dad squeezes his eyes shut. The poker dips.

A faint thud on the porch railing. Another. Like someone brushing past. Or climbing it.

"He's coming to the front," Mae breathes.

All three candles bow toward the door—as if pulled.

Mom lets out a thin, terrified moan.

Dad straightens, not as a father, but as a man who knows exactly who waits outside.

"Everyone stay back."

Dara steps toward him—not touching, but aligned. Dad doesn't push her away.

Footsteps creak across the porch.

Slow. Measured. Intentional.

The doorknob twitches.

Once.

Mom whimpers.

It twitches again. Then turns—not fully. Just enough to prove someone is holding it.

Dad lifts the poker. "Leave," he says, voice shaking but steady enough to sound like authority. "Whoever you are—leave."

A pause. The storm hushes. The flame nearest the door flutters.

Then—

a soft knock.

Not a threat. A request.

tap.

Dad stiffens, breath caught. The sound lands somewhere deep in him.

tap.

Dara watches only him.

"He knows you're awake."

Dad's face folds—not in fear.

In recognition.

Another gentle knock. A childhood rhythm.

Mom cries harder. "Ray, don't open it. Don't you dare."

Dad doesn't move toward the door.

But he doesn't move away.

The knob turns again. Harder. The latch strains.

Mae squeezes my arm until it hurts.

Dara steps closer. "He remembers you."

Dad swallows. His eyes shine. Whatever he remembers, he's spent a lifetime outrunning.

The knock comes again—

tap... tap...

like an unfinished sentence.

Dad whispers, "I can't do this again."

Dara answers, voice soft and absolute. "Then don't make him ask twice."

Wind slams the house. The doorknob stops turning.

But the presence hasn't left.

It's waiting.

The house holds still. The storm holds still.

And for the first time, I understand:

We're not being attacked.

Someone is being confronted.

And it's my father.

Dad's breaths come shallow, too quick. He looks decades older—like time finally caught him.

Another knock at the back window. Then another. Not frantic. Just reminding.

Dara shifts subtly toward the hall, positioning herself between Dad and what hunts memory.

Mom's voice splinters. "Raymond… please… sit down."

He can't.

He's locked in place.

"He trusted me," Dad whispers. "He was scared. And I left him."

The storm slams the west wall, shaking the glass.

Dara's voice is steady. "You didn't know."

Dad's jaw trembles. "I knew enough."

A scraping sound drags across the siding—slow, deliberate—moving toward the living room window.

Mom collapses into the couch, crying silently.

Mae grips my hand. "Why now?"

"Because you're all back," Dara says.

The scraping stops.

A soft, familiar thud.

A presence leaning in.

Dad steps forward before catching himself.

"Raymond—no!" Mom begs.

He freezes.

The candles flicker in different directions. The pressure in the room thickens. The Quiet in me rises, instinctive, bracing, smoothing the air like a shield.

Dara narrows her eyes at the window. "He wants you to look."

Dad's face twists. "I can't."

"You don't have to," she murmurs. "He already knows you're here."

A tender knock touches the glass.

Dad breaks—not with tears, but with memory.

"He was a good kid," he whispers. "He just wanted"-

He stops. He doesn't know if we deserve the truth.

Silence again. Awful, listening silence.

Mom stares at the candles. "Nobody opens anything. Nobody."

"No one is opening a door," Dad agrees, voice shredded. "I know that."

He holds the poker tighter—not for protection, but for courage.

Dara steps closer to the center of the room—the only warmth we have left.

"He won't leave yet," she says.

Mom's voice wavers. "Why?"

Dara's answer is quiet. Final.

"He hasn't made his point."
The window gives the faintest rattle.
Dad whispers, "I hear you. I hear you this time."
The storm groans. The house shifts.
But the presence stays.
Hovering. Listening. Waiting.
Chapter nineteen holds its breath with the rest of us.

CHAPTER TWENTY(AON)—THE HOUSE AFTER

The house does not relax.

It does something else—eases, maybe, the way a body does after a long-held breath has finally been let go, but before sleep is possible.

No one speaks for a while. Not because there is nothing to say, but because saying anything would put shape around what just happened, and none of us are ready to give it edges yet.

The fire has burned low. Not out—just quieter. The sound it makes now is different, more inward than bright.

I notice the small things first. The way the clock in the kitchen has resumed ticking, loud in the absence of voices. The way the couch cushion has shifted where my father sat, like it remembers his weight. The way the hallway doesn't feel quite as narrow as it did an hour ago.

Not kinder. Just altered.

Mae pulls the blanket higher over her shoulders. My mother smooths the fringe without realizing she's doing it, the same motion she used when we were children and something had frightened us but couldn't be named.

Dara does not move.

She sits where she is, head slightly tilted, listening— not outward, but inward, as if she's waiting for the aftersound of something important.

I think, absurdly, of how houses used to be blessed. Not with words, but with pauses. With people standing quietly inside them, acknowledging that something had passed through and might leave a residue.

If the house is aware of us, it does not show it now.

If it remembers what was said, it keeps that memory to itself.

When I finally stand, the floorboard beneath my foot creaks—not in warning, not in complaint.

Just recognition.

CHAPTER TWENTY(DHÀ)— THE HOURS WE HELD

The storm eases without ceremony.

There is no clean break—no moment where the wind stops and everyone exhales at once. It thins instead. Pulls back from the windows. Leaves behind a quiet that feels borrowed, as if it could be reclaimed at any moment.

No one suggests sleeping.

We stay where we are. Blankets knotted around shoulders. Mugs cooling on tables. The house no longer groans, but it doesn't relax either. It feels used. Like a room after an argument where nothing was resolved, only postponed.

My father stands at the window with his hands braced on the sill. Not looking out—listening. His posture is strange to me: not fearful, not defensive. Just held. Like someone who has reached the far edge of what he can outrun.

Every few minutes, he shifts his weight. Rolls his shoulders. As if carrying something invisible that refuses to settle.

My mother has organized the living room without announcing it. Couch cushions straightened. Candles re-centered. Chairs placed with intention, all of us kept within the same sightline like she said earlier—*so we can see each other*. Her jaw is tight. She doesn't sit. She watches the house as if daring it to contradict her.

Mae refolds a blanket that doesn't need it. Smooths it. Then smooths it again. Her movements are careful, domestic, deliberately small. Every so often she glances toward the hallway and then away, as if refusing to finish a thought.

Dara sits cross-legged on the floor near the fireplace. Not close to anyone. Not far either. Still enough that the candlelight barely reaches her face. She doesn't check doors or windows. She doesn't pace. If she hears anything, she doesn't show it.

The house breathes around us.

It's faint, but I feel it—an unevenness in the air, like pressure moving through ribs that aren't mine. I don't say anything. I've learned the cost of naming things too early.

A log settles in the fireplace with a soft, final sound. My mother flinches despite herself. Mae's hand tightens around the edge of the blanket. My father doesn't move.

Minutes pass. Or longer.

At some point, my father picks up the Bible again—not to read. He holds it closed, fingers resting in the cracked leather. Traces a line near the spine the way you might touch an old scar. He doesn't look at any of us while he does it.

I notice that when his thumb pauses, the house seems to pause with him.

Then he exhales, slow and measured, and the quiet returns to its earlier shape.

Mae murmurs something about coffee. No one answers. My mother shakes her head without looking at her. Too soon. Too dangerous to act like the day has started.

Outside, dawn hasn't arrived yet. The light pressing against the windows is dull and metallic, like the world hasn't decided whether to move forward.

I watch the hallway.

Nothing moves there—not really. No sound. No shift of boards. Just a sense that the space is aware of us. Not curious. Just… noting.

I think of long drives when the car goes silent and everyone stares through their own piece of glass, suspended between where they've been and where they're going. This feels like that. A pause that won't resolve itself unless someone forces it.

My mother checks the door lock again. Once. Then a second time. Her fingers linger there longer than necessary.

"We'll talk when it's light," she says, not quite to anyone.

My father nods, though his eyes remain on the window.

Mae finally sits, tucking her feet beneath her, shoulders hunched as if bracing against cold that isn't there.

Dara doesn't move.

Neither does the house.

Time stretches thin, held in our bodies instead of the clock. Whatever happened tonight hasn't finished passing through us yet. It hasn't decided what it's going to leave behind.

And I understand—without knowing how—that this waiting matters.

That staying awake together is part of it.

That something has shifted, even if nothing else happens.

The house listens.

So do we.

CHAPTER TWENTY-ONE(AON)—THE MORNING AFTER

Morning comes slowly—like something unsure it should return.

The house shifts from black to bruised-blue. Frost feathers the windows. Candles have burned down to stubs, and the fire is nothing but pale ash.

Sometime before dawn, the power blinked back on—a click, a hum, the refrigerator joining the quiet as if nothing unusual happened.

None of us slept.

We stayed wrapped in blankets on couches and chairs, afraid that moving would wake something still listening. The air feels bruised. I smooth the heaviness down the way I always do when the room carries more emotion than it can hold.

The house feels… tired. Not safe.

Something in the air twitches against me—thin, unsettled—and the Quiet rises on instinct before I push it back down.

Mae stretches beside me on the couch. "I swear I aged eight years."

"You needed it," I say.

"Dad aged twenty."

We look at him in the recliner—elbows on knees, head bowed, hands clasped so tightly his knuckles shine. He looks like he's trying to hear something only he knows how to hear.

Mom moves around the kitchen with brittle purpose, opening cabinets that don't hold what we need. She moves like she does after funerals—if her hands stay busy, maybe the world will hold together.

She fills the kettle instead. Sets it on the stove. Waits.

Dara stands at the window.

Not looking out.

Her head tilts the way it did last night, like she's tracking something the rest of us can't hear anymore.

Just standing. Listening.

The snow has stopped, but dawn hasn't fully arrived. The light is thin and metallic.

Mae leans in. "We need to get out of this house."

"We will," I say. "When the road opens."

"I don't mean the road."

Before I can reply, a soft crack comes from the back of the house.

Not loud. Not sudden.

A temperature shift. Wood settling.

And yet every one of us freezes.

Dad lifts his head slowly. His eyes look darker than usual. "He's gone," he says quietly.

A silence settles so heavy it feels physical.

Mae whispers, "Are you sure?"

"For now."

For now is the worst answer.

Mom returns with the empty coffeepot, then stops herself. Sets it down. Reaches for a mug instead. "Storm nights do things to the mind," she says too brightly. "We'll feel better once we eat."

"That wasn't the storm," Dara says softly from the window.

Mom flinches. "Enough."

Dad doesn't correct Dara.

He didn't last night either.

Mae whispers, "Does Dad think it was really him?"

"I think he thinks it was something," I say.

Dara turns from the window, her eyes sharp. "He'll come back when the sun goes down."

Mom jerks at the kettle, splashing hot water onto her wrist. She hisses once, sharp and small, then presses a towel against the skin.

"Dara," she says, breath tight, "get your coat. You're leaving with us today."

"We're not leaving," Dara replies. "Not until he's finished."

A chill moves through me—because she doesn't sound afraid.

Dad rubs his face with both hands, slow and tired. "Sit," he says. "I need to tell you something."

Mom stiffens. "Ray—"

Dara closes her eyes like she already knows.

We all sit.

The house stills.

Dad takes a breath.

"It wasn't the first time he knocked."

The whole morning tilts.

CHAPTER TWENTY-ONE(DHÀ) — WHAT DIDN'T LEAVE

Mom sinks into a chair. The mug trembles in her hand.

Dara sits on the floor near the cold fireplace, cross-legged, bracing herself.

Mae rubs her face. "So this boy—the one last night—isn't the one from when I was a teenager?"

Dad shakes his head. "No."

Mom whispers, "But both on our land."

"Yes."

The truth settles like dust—fine, unavoidable.

Mae stares at him. "Why didn't you ever tell us?"

"What good would it have done?" Dad says softly. "You were kids. And I convinced myself the house was the problem. Leaving it behind… felt like fixing it."

Mom's voice cracks. "Raymond… you should have told me."

He looks away. "I was ashamed."

A faint sound shifts outside.

Snow. Maybe.

Or not.

Dara doesn't turn from the window. "He's not far."

"Stop it," Mom snaps. "Enough of these riddles."

"It's not riddles," Dara says. "Some things don't go back to sleep just because the sun comes up."

Dad's silence confirms it.

Mae steps back. "We're leaving. As soon as the plow comes—"

Dad shakes his head. "We may not get that choice."

Mom's voice rises. "Why not?"

Dad's eyes move to the window. "Because it's not about the house."

Dara nods once.

Mom whispers, "Then what *is* it about?"

Dad answers with a breath that sounds heavier than the storm. "It's about me. There are things families carry," he says. "Some we pass down without meaning to."

Mom presses a hand to her chest. "Don't say that."

"What does that mean?" Mae asks.

Dad's eyes lower. "It's not what I did. It's what I allowed."

Mom whispers, "You're frightening us."

Dara speaks gently. "He doesn't mean allowed like permission."

Dad swallows. "I mean allowed like failed to stop."

A hush settles so deep it feels like the air thickens.

Mae's voice trembles. "Dad… tell us the truth."

Dad doesn't look at any of us. He stares at the fireplace ash.

"There were things happening on this land," he says slowly. "Before we bought it. Before all of you were born."

Mom pleads, "Ray, stop—"

"I'm not talking about the owners," he continues.

Mae frowns. "Then who?"

Dara answers for him.

"Family."

Mom shakes her head. "No."

Dad nods.

"Yes."

Mae's voice cracks. "Our family?"

"Not all," Dad says. "But some."

Mom's breath stutters.

Dara murmurs, "He wasn't the first boy to knock."

Mom snaps, "Dara Leanne, stop it."

"He was just the first one who asked nicely," Dara says.

The room freezes.

Mae whispers, "Dad… what happened to him?"

Dad's voice thins. "He didn't live long. And he survived less."

Mom covers her mouth. "Raymond—"

Dad continues. "I was twelve. I couldn't stop what was happening. But I could've helped him that night."

His face folds.

"And I didn't."

The house gives a low groan, as if remembering.

Mae whispers, "He was younger than we were?"

Dad nods. "Yes."

Dara's voice softens. "He was small."

A faint shift moves under the floorboards.

Mom gasps. "I thought you said he was gone."

"For now," Dad murmurs.

Mae grabs my arm. "Claire… what does he want?"

For a moment I think of Hallie—how she would say the air is changing shape, shifting in pieces we can't see.

Dad answers without hesitation.

"Recognition."

Dara whispers, "And he'll want more tonight."

Mom shakes her head. "We won't be here tonight."

Dara looks at her with sympathy. "Leaving won't change anything."

Dad's voice is quiet. "He followed me before."

Mae stares. "Dad—how long?"

Dad looks hollow. "Since the listing went up."

Mom nearly collapses. "Raymond—"

Mae whispers, "Then he was waiting."

Dad nods.

A soft knock comes from beneath the floorboards.

The Quiet in me flinches—as if whatever is beneath us knows exactly where to find it.

Tap.

We all freeze.

Dad closes his eyes.

"He wants me to answer him."

Another *tap.*

Mae begins to cry.

Dad whispers, "I hear you. I'm here."

The knock stops.

The house exhales.

And morning doesn't feel like morning anymore.

By the time Dad begins speaking again, the house feels like a witness—long-suffering, patient, unwilling to let us forget.

The house feels warmer now, though no one has touched the thermostat. It's the kind of warmth that comes after a truth breaks open—heavy, unsettled.

Dad sits again, not because he's calm, but because the memory has taken something out of him. Mae curls on the couch, knees pulled close, bracing herself. Mom clutches the quilt in her lap like it's a life vest.

Dara stands quietly, watching Dad with the still focus of someone who already knows the shape of the story.

Something in the air between us hums faintly, a pressure I smooth down without thinking—like settling dust before it gathers.

I sit closest to him. Because I sense he needs someone to speak toward.

He takes a breath.

"When you're young," he says, "you think everything that happens is your fault. You don't understand that the world existed before you."

His eyes drift toward a past none of us lived with him.

"His name was Louis."

The name settles into the room like a soft bruise.

"He was ten," Dad continues. "Maybe eleven. Small. Quiet. Nervous. His father wasn't kind. He lived close enough that walking onto our property didn't require a reason

— he came the way people do when no one ever asks what they're doing there."

Mom's eyes close. She already knows what that means.

Mae whispers, "So he came to you?"

"He came most evenings," Dad says. "Scratching at the back door. Never knocking. Just… checking if someone was there."

I swallow. "He trusted you."

Dad's eyes shine. "I think I was the only one he trusted."

Dara steps closer, confirming it without words.

"That night," Dad says, "was colder than most. Mama told me to stay in bed. If I opened the door again, she said I'd catch pneumonia."

He pauses.

"And I heard him," he says quietly. "Scratching."

Mom looks like she might break. "Raymond…"

"I was twelve," Dad says. "I thought he'd go home. I didn't know he wasn't safe there."

Mae wipes her face. "Dad… you didn't know."

"I heard him say my name," Dad whispers. "Soft. Scared. Just once."

Something flickers at the edges of my vision—like the air breaking into tiny squares before settling again. Hallie always said the world did that when someone spoke a truth they'd buried too long.

The silence presses in.

"I lay there," Dad says, "pretending to sleep. He walked away. And he never made it home."

Mom presses both hands to her mouth.

Dara nods slowly. "And the family never told the truth."

Dad shakes his head. "Not then. Not ever. His body wasn't found for two weeks."

Mae makes a small sound. "Dad… that wasn't your fault."

He finally meets her eyes. "He asked me not to leave him alone."

A faint shift travels beneath the floorboards.

Mom stiffens. "Raymond—"

Dad lowers his voice. "And I did."

The boards answer with a soft groan, like something acknowledging the sentence.

Dara kneels, placing her hand against the warmest part of the floor.

"He's listening," she murmurs. "He always was."

Mom whispers, "No…"

"He's been waiting a long time," Dara says gently.

Mae grabs my arm. "Dad—what does he want right now?"

Dad answers without hesitation.

"For me to stop pretending he didn't matter."

A soft knock rises from beneath the boards.

tap.

Mae covers her ears. "Make it stop—please—"

Dad closes his eyes. His voice shakes, but it holds. The air tightens, and I feel it move through me—like the house is breathing through my ribs.

"I hear you," he whispers. "I'm here."

The knock stills.

The house releases one long, aching breath.

Mom wipes her face. "Raymond… is that it? Is that all he needed?"

Dad shakes his head. "No. That's only part of it."

A quiet tremor runs along the floor again—subtle, like someone shifting their weight.

"He's not angry," Dara says. "He's hurt. And lost."

Mae whispers, "Dad… how long has he followed you?"

Dad takes a long breath. "Since the listing went up."

Mom stares at him. "Raymond… he came back for you?"

Dad nods. "He always came to me."

Another faint sound comes from the hallway—not a knock, not a scrape—just presence.

Dara closes her eyes, listening. "He's moving. Checking the rooms."

Mae backs away. "Why?"

Dad's answer is soft.

"He's looking for a place he remembers."

Silence settles again—uneasy, expectant.

"What happens now?" Mae asks.

Dad rubs his eyes. "We wait. Until he shows what he needs next."

Mom looks around helplessly. "And we just… sit here?"

"For now," Dad says.

The house goes quiet again, listening to itself.

Outside, the storm thins toward daylight.

CHAPTER TWENTY-THREE— THE SPACE BETWEEN

No one says it out loud, but the house has changed its posture.

Not moved. Not woken. Just… angled itself differently, like a person who has shifted their weight and is now listening with their whole body.

Morning light presses weakly through the windows, pale and undecided. It doesn't chase the dark away so much as negotiate with it. The floorboards hold last night the way wood holds heat—reluctantly, unevenly.

Dad sits at the table with his hands folded around a mug he hasn't lifted. The coffee has gone untouched long enough to film over. He stares at the grain in the wood as if it might say something if he looks long enough.

Mom moves through the kitchen without a destination. She straightens a chair that doesn't need it. Picks up a spoon. Sets it down again. Her movements are precise in the way people get when they're afraid of what happens if they stop moving.

Mae leans against the counter, arms crossed tight, eyes tracking everything and nothing. She's watching for something to break. Or to announce itself.

Dara stays near the hallway.

Not blocking it.

Not guarding it.

Just there—like a line drawn quietly across a page.

No one asks her why.

The house settles once, a small internal shift, the sound of something old adjusting to a truth that's been set down where it can no longer be ignored.

I feel it before I understand it.

A thinning in the air. Not emptiness—focus. Like the space between two notes held just long enough to make the next one inevitable.

Dad exhales slowly. "It's quieter."

Mae stiffens. "Don't say that."

"I don't mean safe," he says quickly. "I just mean… waiting."

That word lands heavier than the others.

Mom turns from the sink. "Waiting for what?"

No one answers her.

Because we all know better than to ask a question that already has a shape.

The hallway doesn't look different. Same pale walls. Same narrow stretch of floor that's carried us from room to room without comment for years. And yet—something about it has claimed attention. Like a place you pass every day until the moment you don't.

I take one step closer without meaning to.

Not toward the end. Just nearer.

The air tightens—not sharply, not painfully. More like a held breath.

Dara tilts her head. "Easy," she murmurs, not warning me away so much as reminding me I don't need to rush.

"I'm not," I say.

It's true.

I'm not being pulled forward.

I'm being allowed to notice.

Dad's chair creaks as he shifts. "I used to think if I didn't look too hard, things would stay where they were."

Mae's voice is thin. "Did it work?"

"For a while," he says. "Long enough to believe it had."

The house responds—not with sound, exactly, but with pressure. A subtle inward draw, like the walls leaning closer to hear what comes next.

Mom presses her fingers to her temple. "I don't like this. I don't like how it feels like the house is… involved."

Dara answers gently. "It always was."

The words aren't an accusation. Just a correction.

Another quiet shift runs through the floorboards. This one closer. Intentional.

Not movement.

Recognition.

I become aware—suddenly, distinctly—of the space behind me. Not occupied, not empty. Attentive. The same awareness you feel when you realize someone is standing just out of sight, waiting for permission to speak.

I don't turn.

I don't need to.

The Quiet in me lifts—not spreading, not pressing, just arranging things so they can be understood without panic. It smooths the moment the way a hand smooths a wrinkle from fabric, not erasing it, just helping it lie flat.

"He's not going to rush it," Dara says quietly.

Dad swallows. "Neither am I."

That might be the most dangerous promise in the room.

Mae looks at me then, really looks. "You're not afraid."

"I am," I say. "Just not in the way you mean."

The house gives a low, almost imperceptible sound—wood responding to temperature, age, time. An old agreement holding.

Outside, something shifts in the distance. Not approaching. Not leaving.

Waiting.

And for the first time since we arrived, I understand what last night cost the house.

It gave up pretending.

CHAPTER TWENTY-FOUR — THE OWNERS

The house feels watchful. Not hostile—just aware. Like it knows what comes next.

A sound hits the front steps.

Not a tap. Not shifting wood. A footstep.

Mom jumps. "Thank the Lord—maybe the plow or a neighbor—"

But Dad's expression doesn't change.

He isn't relieved. He looks braced.

Before any of us can react, a car door slams outside. Hard. Deliberate.

Dara steps closer to the window, listening the way she listens to the house.

"They're here."

Mom exhales. "The owners. Finally—someone to help."

Dad catches her wrist before she reaches the door.

"Lillian," he says quietly. "Wait."

"Why? We have to let them in."

Dad's voice is steady, almost tired.

"Because they're not surprised."

The doorknob jiggles. Once.

Then a cheerful voice calls out:

"Well hello, house! Mornin'! Storm hit ya pretty good out in these parts!"

Mom forces a smile she doesn't feel. "See? They're checking on us."

But something in the voice doesn't match the words. It's too bright. Too practiced.

The doorknob turns deeper in its socket.

Dara steps sharply between Mom and the door. "Don't open it."

Something thin and metallic lifts in the air, and I smooth it down without meaning to.

Mom snaps, "This is their property, Dara Leanne—"

"They knew he was here," Dara says softly. "Before we did."

A shadow moves past the window. Broad. Unhurried. Surveying.

Mae grips my arm. "Claire… they're right outside the living room."

The woman's voice joins the man's—cheery, syrup-thick.

"Mornin'! We just need t 'check your utilities! Pipes freeze fast out har!"

But her eyes flick—too quickly—toward the guest room hallway.

Dad steps forward as the door swings open.

"Well howdy!" the man booms, stomping snow across the entry mat without looking down.

The floorboards answer with one slow, sinking groan—recognition, not weight.

"Landlord hospitality, no matter the weather!"

The woman steps inside with a bright smile that doesn't touch her eyes.

"We just wanted to check on our favorite guests."

Favorite guests.

As if we've stayed here before. As if they know us.

Mom tries to block their path. "We're fine. Truly. Just a long night."

"Oh, we won't be but a minute," the woman says.

She's already slipping past.

Not toward the kitchen. Toward the hallway. Toward the room where we heard Louis move.

Dad steps forward. "There's nothing to check."

The man laughs—a bright, empty sound.

"Well now, let us be the judge of that!"

He wanders the kitchen, tapping baseboards, scanning floors.

Too observant. Too familiar.

Mae whispers, "They're looking for something."

Dara lowers her voice. "They're looking for someone."

From down the hall, the woman calls out:

"Hey, hon? You might want to see this."

Dad closes his eyes. Just once.

Like he already knows.

The man excuses himself from us with a polite nod and strolls toward her voice.

Mom's nails dig into my arm. "Claire—what are they doing?"

"They're checking where Louis went," Dara says.

Dad sinks heavily into a kitchen chair. "They know everything that happens in this house."

The woman's voice floats back from the guest room—soft, pleased.

"Well… looks like he was awake after all."

Her words aren't meant for any of us.

The man answers, lower.

"There he is."

A chill moves through the house—wall to wall, floor to ceiling.

And just like that, we understand:

The owners aren't checking on us.

They're checking on Louis.

The boy Dad didn't answer. The boy who never made it home. The boy whose memory clings to the walls like frost.

The boy they've known about all along.

And suddenly I see it clearly—

They were never afraid of Louis.

They were waiting on him.

And now he's answering.

CHAPTER TWENTY-FIVE—WHAT I MISSED

The woman's words linger in the hallway long after she speaks them.

"There he is…"

Not loud. Not surprised.

Almost… satisfied.

Mom grips my arm so tight her nails bite through the fabric. Mae stops breathing beside me. Dad goes utterly still, like his body is bracing for something he's spent his whole life avoiding.

Dara steps forward, not toward the woman—but between Dad and the hallway, like she already knows what's coming.

The man doesn't hurry. His boots brush the floorboards as he walks down the hall to join his wife, each step too calm, too confident. Like this is routine for them.

I can't see into the guest room from where I stand.

But I don't have to.

I feel it.

A shift in the air. A pressure.

A trace drawn there—recently, quietly, intentionally.

And I'm the only one in the house not shaking.

I don't know why that hits me so suddenly, but it does.

Mom is trembling. Mae can't seem to exhale. Dad looks like a man who's run out of years to hold anything back.

But me?

I'm steady.

Not brave. Not numb.

Just… knowing.

The intuition I've lived with my whole life—too sensitive, too odd, too much for most people—rises like a second heartbeat. The room sharpens. The air clears. And instantly, I can feel what the others can't.

What followed the warmth last night. What brushed the walls. What the owners are standing in the doorway to see.

I close my eyes for half a second.

Gosh, I wish I could talk to Sam.

Not because he would magically fix this—not because he'd believe everything happening in this house—but because Sam always listened when I talked about things no one else took seriously.

The flickers I see in people. The truths I hear under their voices. The way a room feels different before anything actually happens.

He never called it superstition. He never asked me to justify it.

He just… accepted it.

And right now, surrounded by family who are either terrified or in denial, I feel more alone than I have in years.

Sam would say, "Tell me what you're sensing, Claire."

No one here asks.

No one even looks at me—except Dara.

She turns her head slightly, eyes narrowing, as if she feels that same shift in me that I feel in her. Like she knows I'm tuned into this house in a way the others aren't.

The woman's voice comes again, from the guest room doorway—light, almost lilting.

"Well isn't that something…"

Dad inhales sharply at that sound.

Not fear—recognition.

Mom whispers, "Raymond, what are they doing?"

"They're looking for signs," I say quietly.

Everyone turns to me then.

They weren't ready to hear my voice, but it's too late.

I've already seen what they missed.

The owners aren't shocked. They're not confused. They're not even scared.

They're checking.

Mapping.

Reading.

Tracking something that moved last night—and moved again this morning.

They knew exactly where to go the second they walked inside.

Dara shifts closer to me, her voice low. "Claire… what do you feel?"

The question lands like a warm hand on a frozen shoulder.

Because she's the only one who's ever asked me that in this entire house.

I take a slow breath, letting the truth rise.

"He's not in that room," I whisper. "But he was."

Dad flinches. Mom gasps. Mae's eyes go wide and raw.

"And the owners," I continue, "aren't checking the house."

I look toward the hall. Toward the guest room where the woman stands smiling at a presence we can't see.

"They're checking his trail."

The house creaks once, low and long, like it approves of the truth finally being said out loud.

And somewhere—behind the walls, beneath the floorboards, in the warm places where breath gathers—

Something shifts again.

Waiting for someone to finally understand.

The woman's silhouette shifts slightly in the guest-room doorway. She's not bending or kneeling or checking the pipes like she claimed she would.

She's standing very still.

Looking down at something on the floor.

Something at a child's height.

The man joins her, his voice dropping into that too-calm register that people use when they think they're whispering, but want to be overheard.

"Well now… that's new."

A cold ripple slides across the room.

Dad steps forward before he can stop himself. "What are you looking at?"

The woman doesn't answer. She tilts her head, studying the corner of the room like she's examining a footprint in soft earth.

I can't see what she sees.

But I can feel it.

A pull passed through that room last night.

Something small. Something determined.

Something that hadn't been in that hallway for years—until we came back.

Dara shifts beside me, her breath hitching. "Claire, don't go closer."

But I'm already moving.

I don't know why I do it—only that I have to. Something in my intuition pulls me toward the hall like a string tugging at my ribs.

Mom grabs my wrist. "Claire—no."

"It's okay," I whisper.

She doesn't believe me, but she lets go.

Dad steps aside to let me pass, his face ashen. His voice is barely audible. "Don't look too hard."

But that's the thing.

I've been looking hard my whole life.

The hallway feels colder, narrower, as I walk toward the guest room. The woman turns her head slightly when she hears me coming. Her smile doesn't drop, but it… changes.

Flattens. Sharpens.

Like she didn't expect me to be the one who walked forward.

The man glances at her, then at me, eyebrows lifting just a fraction.

"Well now," he says softly. "Brave one, aren't you?"

Bravery has nothing to do with it.

I stop in the doorway beside them.

The guest room is dim, the curtains pulled tight, the air heavy with cold that doesn't match the rest of the house. The bed is neatly made. The dresser untouched.

The floor—

The floor is what catches me.

Near the far wall, in the thin dust that the storm air pushed under the window, there's a small shape.

A mark.

Not quite a footprint. Not quite a handprint.

Something in between—like a small palm dragged across the floor as something tried to pull itself upright.

A smear of movement preserved in dust.

A child's movement.

My chest tightens.

The woman watches my face closely as I see it. "You understand it, don't you?" she murmurs.

I don't look at her.

I can't.

Because the second I see that faint shape, something clicks inside me—clean, sharp, inevitable.

He wasn't wandering. He wasn't lost. He wasn't confused.

He was looking for someone.

For Dad. For warmth. For safety. For an answer he never got.

The woman kneels, brushing her fingers near the mark without touching it. "He always tries this room first," she says conversationally, like she's talking about a raccoon or a leaky faucet. "Something about the way the heat settles."

The man chuckles under his breath. "Poor little thing's stuck in his old patterns."

Dara stiffens. "Don't talk about him like that."

The woman rises slowly, eyes flicking toward Dara with something like amusement. "He's not yours to defend."

"No," I say quietly. "He's Dad's."

They look at me then—really look—and something in the woman's expression changes.

Not fear. Not guilt.

Recognition.

"Intuitive, are you?" she asks.

My breath catches.

Sam's voice flickers through my mind:

Tell me what the room is telling you, Kitten.

I lift my chin. "Sometimes."

"That's a family trait," the man says.

I swallow. "Not in your family."

They both smile at that.

Not kindly.

The woman steps out of the room, brushing past me as she returns to the hall. "You should leave the mark where it is," she says lightly. "He'll need it tonight."

Mae's voice cracks from the living room. "Tonight? What happens tonight?"

The woman pauses at the end of the hall and turns, offering Mae a smile so sweet it curdles the air.

"Why… the same thing that always happens."

Mae pales.

Dad grips the back of the couch like he's holding on to something slipping from his grasp.

The man strolls past me toward the tiny entryway, calling over his shoulder, "We'll give y'all space. Wouldn't want to interrupt any… visitations."

The woman is the last to step through the door. She pauses on the threshold, her eyes drifting once more to the baseboards.

Then she looks at me.

At me, not Dad.

"Your gift will be trouble," she says gently. "But it'll be the thing that saves him."

Before I can speak, she adds:

"And one day? It'll save more than him."

She smiles. Soft. Wrong. Knowing.

Then she steps outside and closes the door behind her.

The house settles.

The warmth shifts.

Something moves—behind the walls, toward the mark in the dust.

And the truth hits me like a cold wind:

Louis knows I saw him.

And he's coming back for the one thing he never had—

Someone who listens.

The door clicks shut behind the owners, and for a moment none of us moves. It feels like the whole house is holding itself still, waiting to see what we'll do now that the people who pretend to "manage" this land have walked away.

Mom is the first to break. She rushes toward Dad, gripping his arm. "We're leaving. I don't care. I don't care what they said. I don't care what they think they know. We are leaving."

Dad doesn't look at her. He's staring down the hallway toward the guest room, toward the faint smear in the dust—toward the place where the boy dragged his small hand across the floor.

"We can't," he says softly.

Mom stares at him like he's lost his mind. "What do you mean we can't?"

Dad's eyes are tired but clear. "If we leave now, he'll follow."

Mae's breath catches in her throat. "Dad… please stop saying he follows us. Please."

"It's the truth," Dad murmurs.

But the truth isn't the heaviest thing in the room. Not anymore.

Because I can feel something else now—something new, something quiet, something unmistakably alive. It's faint… like a shift in air pressure, or the softest tug behind my sternum.

A recognition. A turning-toward.

Dara sees it the second my breath changes.

She steps closer, eyes narrowing with understanding. "Claire," she whispers. "Did you feel that?"

Mae stiffens. "Feel what?"

Mom looks at me like she wants me to say no. Like she needs me to say it's nothing.

But lying won't help anyone.

"He knows I saw him," I say quietly.

The room goes dead still.

Dad closes his eyes like the words hit him in the place where his guilt lives deepest.

Mom presses both hands over her mouth. "Oh Gosh… oh Gosh…"

Mae backs up, shaking her head. "No. No, Claire, don't say that. Don't make this worse."

But it's already happening.

Down the hall, a subtle warmth drifts from the guest-room doorway. Like someone just breathed out. Not cold. Not icy. Warm.

Dara whispers, almost reverently, "He's drawn to you."

I feel my pulse thud once and then settle, steady and low. "Why?"

"Because you're listening," Dara murmurs.

Mom lets out a sob. "Claire—please—stop responding to this. You don't have to… you don't have to feel these things."

But I do. I always have.

It's not something I turn on and off. It's built into me. Inherited. Heavy. Unavoidable.

And now it's awake.

A sudden ache rises in my chest—unexpected, sharp, overwhelming.

Sam. I wish he were here. I wish I could hear his voice. I wish I could tell him what I'm feeling and have him say: *Okay. Tell me everything. Start from the beginning.*

Because Sam would believe me. Or if he didn't, he'd try. He'd listen with that quiet, steady way he always did—as if my intuition wasn't strange or dramatic, but a compass that had never once pointed wrong.

And I wouldn't feel so alone in this room.

Dad sinks into a chair, rubbing the back of his neck. "We should sit. We should… we should think."

"No," I say softly.

All eyes whip toward me.

"We don't have time to think."

Mom's voice shakes. "Claire—please—don't start talking like Dara."

But Dara's face lights with something like relief. "She's not talking like me. She's talking like herself."

Mae looks between us, terrified. "Why? Why don't we have time?"

Because the warmth in the hallway thickens. Because the house itself feels tighter. Because something with small hands and an old ache is moving again—closer, just a little closer—drawn to recognition like moths to lamplight.

And because the owners didn't lie: Tonight will be worse. Much worse.

I take a slow breath, grounding myself in the floorboards, in the moment, in the deep intuitive pulse that has always lived in me.

"We don't have time," I repeat, "because he's already coming back."

The house creaks once, a long, low groan. Like agreement. Or warning.

And as the sound fades, I swear I feel it again—that faint, warm brush just behind my ribs.

A presence learning me.

A child remembering a door that was once shut in his face— and hoping this time…

someone might open it.

The warmth in the hallway grows stronger. Not enough to feel like heat, not enough to warm the skin—just enough to make the air feel occupied.

Mom curls in on herself on the couch. "This is insane… this is absolutely insane. We shouldn't have come. We shouldn't have rented this place. I knew—Raymond, I knew—"

Dad isn't listening. He's staring down the hallway again, face clenched in something between dread and resignation.

Mae starts pacing in sharp, tight lines. "We need to go. I don't care if he follows. I don't care if the roads are blocked. I don't care—Claire, stop saying things like that. STOP it."

Dara steps between Mae and the hall, her voice low. "Yelling won't help."

Mae turns on her. "Oh, you would know, wouldn't you? You always know things you can't explain!"

"Because I've lived it," Dara says simply.

Something softens in the house at that sentence. A subtle shift. A breath.

Mom sobs into her hands. "This is tearing us apart. Raymond, SAY something!"

Dad finally looks up—but not at her. At me.

"Claire," he says quietly, "what did you feel?"

For a moment, no one else breathes.

Dara turns toward me as if she already knows how important this is. Mae stops pacing, frozen mid-step. Mom lifts her tear-blurred face.

They're all waiting.

But even with all their eyes on me…

I feel alone.

Sam would sit down, elbows on knees, and ask gently: *What is the house saying?*

And I would tell him. And he would believe me.

I swallow hard. "He… noticed me."

Mae flinches. "STOP. Don't say things like that."

"It's true," I whisper.

Mom sobs harder.

Dad's eyes close, heavy with a sorrow I don't fully understand. "It was going to happen," he murmurs.

"What does that mean?" Mae demands.

Dara answers before he can. "It means he found someone who can hear him."

The room chills.

"What?" I ask, my voice barely air. "Why me?"

Dara steps closer, her expression unreadable but not unkind. "Because you see things as they are. You always have."

"How would you know that?" Mae snaps.

Dara doesn't blink. "Because I was the same way."

Dad lets out a shaky exhale. "She's right."

Mom whispers, horrified, "No… no… not Claire… please, Lord, not Claire…"

But it's too late.

Louis knows I felt him. He knows I saw the mark. He knows I walked forward when everyone else froze.

I feel his awareness now like a soft twinge in the air as the warmth in the hallway pulses once. A small, careful brush. Like a child peeking around a doorframe.

Curious. Hopeful. Drawn.

Not malicious. Just longing.

My throat tightens. "He's close."

Dara nods. "Yes."

Mae shakes her head violently. "NO. No no no—this is CRAZY…"

The house creaks. A single board flexes in the hallway—not like settling, not like age, but like weight shifting.

I turn toward the sound, breath catching.

"Claire," Dara murmurs, "don't move unless he means for you to."

A soft, hesitant warmth radiates from the guest-room threshold.

And then—

a faint brush of air passes my cheek.

Like someone small and scared and hopeful leaned close enough to look at me.

Mom lets out a strangled cry. "CLAIRE—come back here—"

But I don't move.

Because the warmth isn't frightening.

It's sad.

It's the same feeling I used to get when Sam would look at me across a room full of people who didn't understand either of us.

Seen. Recognized. Found.

Louis isn't reaching for Dad this time.

He's reaching for me.

"Why is he drawn to her?" Mae whispers, terrified.

Dad's voice is rough. "Because she's listening."

And Dara adds softly, "And because she won't lie to him."

CHAPTER TWENTY-SEVEN—WHAT THE HOUSE ALLOWS

The house does not move, but something inside it rearranges itself.

Not furniture. Not walls. Something less visible. A pressure shift. The kind you feel in your ears before weather changes, or before someone says a thing that cannot be unsaid.

I stand near the hallway, not quite in it, not fully out. The air here is warmer than the rest of the room. Not heat—occupation. As if the space has been claimed without sound or permission.

No one speaks.

Mom has gone very still on the couch, her hands folded in her lap too tightly, knuckles pale. Mae hovers near the window, her reflection doubled against the glass—herself and someone thinner, more uncertain, standing just behind her. Dad sits with his shoulders rounded forward, staring at the floor like it might finally forgive him if he looks long enough.

Dara watches none of this.

She's watching me.

I feel it without turning. The way you feel a gaze when it's intentional. Measured. Not curious—assessing.

"Don't," she says quietly.

It's not a warning. It's instruction.

"I'm not doing anything," I answer.

"I know," she says. "That's what matters."

The warmth in the hallway pulses once. Subtle. Careful. Like something testing the edges of itself.

I press my fingers lightly against the wall. The paint is cool beneath my skin, the texture faintly rough. Solid. Real. Ordinary. I let myself feel it on purpose, anchoring to the simplest thing available.

The house smells like old fabric and wood that's held heat too long. Somewhere deeper in it, something ticks—pipes, maybe. Or something settling that hasn't settled in years.

I think, briefly, of Sam.

Not his face. Not his voice. Just the way he used to stand beside me in quiet moments, close enough to register, far enough not to crowd. The way he never rushed me when I went still. The way he knew stillness wasn't absence—it was attention.

I miss him with a sharpness that almost breaks my focus.

The hallway answers that feeling, as if it recognizes the shape of it.

I do not step forward.

That seems to matter.

Dara nods once, almost imperceptibly.

The house makes a small sound then—not a creak, not a groan. A shift. Like weight easing from one place to another. It doesn't feel threatening. It feels... deliberate.

Allowing, not advancing.

I understand something then—not in words, not fully. This isn't about crossing over. Not yet. This is about position. About where bodies are placed. About who will move first when movement finally happens.

Louis is not here in the way we've been taught to understand presence.

He is pattern. Memory held tight enough to thicken the air. He is what remains when wanting outlasts time.

And right now, he is watching to see what will be repeated.

No one notices the way my breathing evens out. No one notices the way the room's tension bends slightly, responding to something unspoken being held instead of released.

Except Dara.

"Good," she murmurs.

Mom looks up at that. "What's good?"

Dara doesn't answer her.

The warmth recedes a fraction—not gone, just less centered. As if something has stepped back half a pace, waiting for instruction it doesn't yet trust.

I step away from the hallway first.

Not retreating. Resetting.

The air follows me partway, then stops. Respecting a boundary.

Dad lifts his head, eyes searching my face. "Is it…?"

"No," I say softly. "Not yet."

That answer seems to land with more weight than anything else spoken today.

The house exhales—not relief. Recognition.

We are all still inside it. Still inside the moment. But the shape of what comes next has clarified. The silence no longer feels stalled. It feels staged.

Waiting, yes.

But waiting with direction.

I sit.

The couch creaks beneath me, ordinary and imperfect. Mae glances over, her fear threaded now with something else—uncertainty, maybe. Or the beginning of trust.

Outside, wind moves through the trees, steady and unresolved.

Inside, the house holds.

It does not rush us.

It knows it won't have to.

CHAPTER TWENTY-EIGHT — THE ONE WHO
CALLS

Mom's sobs echo through the living room, sharp and uneven, like she's trying to expel something lodged inside her for decades.

Mae stands rigid near the hallway, arms wrapped around herself. "I don't understand any of this," she whispers. "Why is this happening to us? Why now? Why—Claire, *why* you?"

Because I'm the only one who isn't running.

But I can't say that. Not yet. She'd never forgive me.

Instead, I step slowly toward the hallway, the air warming around me in soft pulses.

Dara moves with me at first—then stops herself. She watches me with a strange mix of fear and recognition, like she's seeing an echo of her own childhood step forward.

Dad wipes his face, panic and guilt warring in him. "He came back because I didn't answer him then. That's why. This is my fault."

"It's not fault," I say softly. "It's unfinished."

A long silence stretches—thin, trembling.

Then Mae snaps.

"This is madness!" she shouts. "We should be calling the sheriff. Or a priest. Or—gosh, I don't know—*anyone* but standing here talking to walls!"

"He's not in the walls," Dara says evenly.

Mae whirls on her. "Stop. I swear to goodness, Dara, if you say one more creepy thing—"

"Mae," Dara cuts in, firm, "he's beside your sister."

Mae's face drains of color.

Mom screams, "No—no no no—stop saying that—"

But Dara isn't wrong.

I feel him.

Not looming. Not threatening.

More like a tug on a sleeve. A child's careful attempt to get someone's attention without being scolded.

Dad staggers forward. "Louis? Son? If you can hear me—"

"Raymond," Dara snaps. "Don't you *dare* address him right now."

Dad freezes like she struck him.

I draw a shaky breath, trying to steady the room. "Why not, Dara?"

She looks at me grimly. "Because he's not steady. He's not formed. He's pieces. He's memory trying to become body. If Ray calls to him now, Louis might follow the wrong tether."

My throat tightens. "What do you mean—wrong tether?"

"If he follows guilt instead of truth," Dara says, "he won't find peace. He'll cling."

Mom lets out a choking sob.

Mae covers her mouth.

And Dad—God help him—sits down like eighty years just dropped onto his shoulders in a single breath.

I want to go to him.

But something stops me.

141

A sound.

Not a tap this time.

A scrape.

Soft. Faint.

Against wood.

I turn slowly toward the baseboards. Toward the guest-room threshold, where that faint warmth keeps blooming.

Dara's voice lowers. "Don't rush. Let him show you."

Another scrape.

My heart thuds once—not fear. Recognition.

Something slides across the floor toward me.

I kneel as it stops at my fingertips.

A button.

Worn smooth. Once blue, now faded toward gray. A tiny thread still clings to the back.

Dad's breath collapses out of him. "Oh… my heavens."

Mom's knees buckle. "Raymond—what is that?"

His face crumples. "His coat. He had a blue coat. His mother sewed those buttons herself. Said she liked blue on him."

Mae whispers, horrified, "Is that… is that his?"

Another scrape answers her—this one from the wall behind me.

Closer.

Dad reaches forward instinctively.

Dara grabs his wrist. "Not yet. Let Claire."

Mom's voice shatters. "Why her? Why is he coming to *her*?"

Because Sam would have listened. Because Sam said my intuition wasn't strange—it was a gift. Because I don't flinch from truth, even when it terrifies me.

Because someone has to see him. And he knows I can.

I lift the button, turning it in my palm. It's warm—as if touched by breath or small fingers.

I close my hand around it. "Louis," I whisper. "I see you."

The house exhales.

The hallway light flickers.

Mom collapses into sobs. "Claire—please—please stop talking to it—"

But I'm not talking to *it*.

I'm talking to a boy who never made it home. Who knocked until his hands went numb. Who waited in the cold. Who died alone.

And who finally—after decades of silence—has someone willing to answer.

A faint pressure brushes my shoulder, gentle as asking permission.

Dad chokes on a sob. "Claire… what does he want?"

I press the button to my chest. "I think," I whisper, "he wants us to see where he went next."

Dara nods. "Yes."

Mae's voice cracks. "Tonight… isn't it?"

Dara glances toward the window. The light is already thinning. Storm clouds are gathering again.

"No," she says. "Before night."

The house creaks sharply—one decisive warning.

Something is coming before dark.

And for the first time, I'm truly afraid.

Not of Louis.

But of what might be coming *with* him.

The house groans again—low, deliberate.

Dara and I hear it the same way. I see it in her eyes. Something is shifting.

Dad wipes his face. "Claire, sweetheart… you don't have to do this. You don't have to let him use you."

"He's not using her," Dara says. "He's trusting her."

Mom shakes, sobbing. "Don't make this normal. Don't—"

"Lillian," Dara says steadily, "do you want him angry?"

Mom goes still. "Angry?"

"He isn't now," Dara says. "But he could be—if we pretend not to hear him. If we repeat what was done to him before."

That silence is thick enough to choke on.

Mae presses her hands to her temples. "Oh my gosh… I can't—"

A soft knock comes again from the baseboard.

tap

…tap

……tap

Calling to me.

Dara inclines her head. "He wants to show you something."

"No!" Mom screams. "Claire—don't you dare—"

Dad catches her arm. "Lillian—stop. We need to see what he needs us to see."

Mom sobs. "Not her. Why her?"

Dad looks at me—grief and clarity braided together. "Because she hears him."

Another tap.

I step toward the hallway.

Not because I'm brave. Not because I want to.

Because something inside me pulls—steady, familiar.

The same pull I felt when Sam used to say, *Go with your gut, Kitten.*

I miss him so badly it hurts.

But I swallow it and keep moving.

The warmth thickens—childlike, tentative.

"Claire," Mom whispers, breaking, "please don't go alone—"

"She's not alone," Dara says.

Dad nods. "We're here."

I reach the doorway.

The mark in the dust is still there—the drag of a small palm.

And beside it, something new.

A faint smear, angled toward the bedframe.

Like a knee slid. Like a small body shifted.

Like a story that never finished being told.

After the calling, the house goes quiet.

Not empty. Not peaceful. Just… held.

The warmth near the hallway thins, retreating the way a tide does—slow, reluctant, leaving its shape behind. I feel it recede like pressure easing from a bruise: not gone, but no longer demanding attention.

Mom sits exactly where she was, eyes red, hands folded too neatly in her lap. She looks smaller now, like something in her finally bent instead of breaking. Mae hasn't moved either. She's watching the floor, jaw tight, counting breaths the way she did when we were kids and scared of thunderstorms.

Dad stands near the chair, both hands braced on its back. He doesn't sit. He doesn't follow me. He looks emptied—like the act of being heard took more out of him than the night itself.

Dara is the only one who seems unchanged.

She tilts her head slightly, listening to the aftermath the way some people listen to echoes. When she speaks, her voice is quieter than before.

"That's enough for now."

"For now," Mae repeats, hollow.

"Yes," Dara says. "For today."

No one argues.

The house ticks softly—pipes cooling, wood contracting, the small sounds of a place that still remembers how to be ordinary. The storm outside has loosened its grip. Wind moves through the trees without urgency.

I hadn't realized how tense my shoulders were until they lower.

The button is still in my hand.

I hadn't dropped it.

I hadn't thought about it either, but it's there—warm against my palm, an anchor I didn't ask for. I curl my fingers around it once, then open them again.

I don't put it away.

That feels important.

Dad notices. Our eyes meet for half a second. There's guilt there. Gratitude too. And something like fear—not of me, but of what this means going forward.

"I don't know what happens next," he says.

I nod. "Neither do I."

That honesty lands easier than reassurance would have.

Outside, light shifts—subtle, gray thinning toward afternoon. Time resumes in small, allowable increments. No one rushes to fill it.

Mom finally exhales. Not a sob. Just air leaving her lungs like she's been holding it since last night. "We'll eat," she says automatically. "Later. When we can."

Mae manages a nod.

Dara's gaze flicks once toward the hallway, then away. Satisfied, or at least settled.

"This isn't finished," she says. "But it's paused."

Paused is something I can live with.

I close my hand again, grounding myself in the small certainty of weight and texture. Somewhere deep in the house, something adjusts—not forward, not closer. Just enough to mark that a boundary has been acknowledged.

Whatever happens next will not arrive unannounced.

Not anymore.

The house stands.

So do we.

CHAPTER THIRTY — THE KEY IN THE CRAWL GAP

Then—under the bed—something glints faintly.

I kneel slowly. A tiny brass object rests just beneath the dust ruffle, as if dropped by a child crawling in fear. A key—old, cold—with a ribbon tied to it, faded plaid torn at the edges.

Dad gasps. "His key… that ribbon… his mother used it on his mittens so he wouldn't lose them."

Mae whispers, "Why is it under the bed?"

Another soft scrape answers her.

Not from under the bed.

From inside the wall to the left of it.

He moved through the crawl gap—the small spaces between rooms, the forgotten places, the parts no one sealed.

Dara closes her eyes, voice trembling. "He used to do that with me."

Mom's head whips around. "WHAT?"

Dara opens her eyes slowly, looking at the wall like she can see straight through it. "I was eight. Sometimes he'd move through the gaps and end up beside my dresser. Some mornings there'd be little things out of place. A marble. A penny. A scrap of ribbon."

Mae looks nauseous. "Why didn't you tell anyone?"

"I did," Dara says. "You all told me I was dreaming."

Dad closes his eyes like her words punch him in the chest.

Mom covers her mouth, tears streaming. "Oh… Dara… oh no…"

Dara doesn't soften. "I learned not to talk about it. Because every time I did, you treated me like I was broken instead of right."

Her eyes meet mine.

"And that's why he likes Claire. She doesn't run from what she knows."

The house hums softly—warm, approving.

I pick up the key, the ribbon brushing my fingers. The metal is cold, but the ribbon is warm—like someone held it moments ago.

Dad whispers, "Claire… what does he want you to see?"

I hold the key to my chest, feeling the ribbon slip between my fingers like a tether. "He wants to show me where he went when he left the door. Not to drag me into it— just to make me understand what he ran from."

The house groans—low, heavy, full of memory.

Mae backs away. "No. No no no—don't say that— don't go there—Claire, STOP—"

But I already know.

Louis isn't trying to scare me. He's trying to lead me.

Dara exhales, reading my face. "He's trying to take you to the woods."

Mom screams, "NO—ABSOLUTELY NOT—"

A sudden, sharp gust hits the side of the house, hard enough to rattle the windowpanes. The wind wasn't blowing a moment ago.

Dad grips the doorway for balance. "The storm's coming back…"

"No," Dara whispers. "That wasn't the storm."

I look toward the window. The sky has gone darker—heavy, dense—like dusk is falling too early.

The key warms in my palm.

Louis is calling.

And night isn't waiting.

The key pulses again—a small beat, almost like a heartbeat. Not magic—just a message, the way an object can hold a child's insistence.

Dara steps closer, her gaze flicking between me and the baseboard. "He's pulling you. Slow now—don't let him rush you."

"I'm not rushing," I whisper.

But I am moving.

My feet shift toward the window without me thinking about it, like something unseen is gently tugging a thread tied around my ribs.

Mom lurches forward. "CLAIRE—NO—"

Dad grabs her before she can reach me. "Lillian—don't—she's okay."

"How can she be okay?!" Mom screams. "She's going TOWARD it!"

Mae starts crying—quiet, panicked sobs. "Why is he choosing her? Why not Dad? Why not Dara? Why Claire—why—"

"Because Claire listens," Dara says, her voice soft but steady as steel. "And because he knows she won't scream at him. He knows she isn't afraid of the truth."

The truth.

That's what the key feels like in my hand—a truth rubbed smooth by time and small hands.

The house groans again—another warning, another memory, another tug.

My footsteps slow near the window. The glass is frosted, the light outside dimming too fast for the time of day.

I touch the window frame carefully.

And suddenly—I ache for Hallie.

It hits me so fast and sharp I gasp. Her face. Her laugh. Her messy hair in the mornings. Her little *love you, Momma* texts when she's anxious or homesick. Our bedtime prayers.

Gosh, I miss my daughter.

I wish she were here—not because she could help, not because she could stop any of this—but because she would know when my voice shakes, and when it doesn't.

Hallie always read my face like a map.

But I am alone in this moment. Sam isn't here to listen. Hallie isn't here to steady me. And my family is splintering in fear behind me.

A soft breath fogs the lower corner of the window.

Child-height.

Mom screams, backing away. "NO—NO—DON'T LOOK—"

But I do.

Because I'm not afraid of him.

A small smudge appears in the fog—not a handprint, not a face—just a single smooth line, drawn slow, like a small finger tracing the glass.

Trying to show me something.

Dara steps beside me. "Claire… he wants you to see outside."

"But what?" I whisper.

"I don't know yet."

The smudge drifts to the right—slow, deliberate— toward the tree line, toward the woods.

Dara inhales sharply. "He's showing you where he walked."

"Walked WHERE?" Mae cries. "Claire—PLEASE stop—"

I take one tiny step closer.

The trees are swaying even though the wind hasn't reached the house. The shadows between the trunks are too dark, too deep.

Then—

Movement.

Not Louis.

Too tall.

Something stands between two trees, watching the house.

My breath stops.

Dara sees it too. Her voice goes razor-thin. "That's not him."

Before Dad can speak, the figure vanishes into the tree line like mist.

Louis's warmth shifts beside me—not fearful, but urgent.

Whatever took him, whatever he ran from—it wasn't just the cold.

The smudge presses into a small circle, then smears downward, like a child crouching before crawling away.

"He's showing you how he left the house," Dara whispers.

The room behind us erupts, but it feels far away.

Louis isn't haunting.

He's pointing.

Leading.

Brave and broken and small.

Dad's hand lands on my shoulder. "Claire—step away from the window."

"I'm okay."

"No," he says, voice cracking. "You're not."

I step back—not from fear, but instinct.

Louis pulls back when I do.

He likes it when I match him.

I set the key gently on the table. It glows faintly—not supernatural, just warmer than metal should be.

Dad notices. "It's reacting to you."

"It's reacting to him," Dara corrects.

Mom paces in a tight circle. "This is dangerous."

Dad closes his eyes. "It's dangerous not to listen."

The woods aren't empty.

Louis is small. Soft. Shy.

The thing out there is none of those.

It watches with a stillness that doesn't belong to anything living.

It wasn't something that followed people. It showed up where something had already been worn thin.

Dad whispers, "Claire… what did you see?"

"Not him."

"What shape?" Dara asks.

"Tall," I say. "Too tall."

Dara nods once.

And then—

The rug shifts.

A hidden crack reveals itself.

A crawl gap.

From beneath it slides a scrap of faded cloth—child-sized, blue once, now the color of old sky.

Then something wooden.

Small.

A toy horse.

Hand-carved.

Dad collapses. "Louis made that. He brought it to me. He said his father didn't want him playing with toys anymore. He asked me to keep it."

His voice breaks completely.

"I told him he was too old for it. I told him he didn't need toys anymore. I told him to stop acting like a baby and go home."

The words land like a body.

Outside, something tall shifts closer.

Louis's warmth flares—urgent, pleading.

Don't let it in.

The toy horse rests in Dara's palm, its tiny legs cracked by time.

Dad sobs. "I sent him away."

And in the woods—

Something listens.

And hunts.

CHAPTER THIRTY-ONE — WHERE HE FELL

The cold still clings to my hands from the floorboard when the woods answer back.

A low, reverberating sound rolls through the trees—not a growl, not a voice, but something like air collapsing, as if the forest itself is bracing for something older than it.

The tall figure steps forward.

One long, deliberate step.

Everyone screams. Even Dad. Even Dara.

But Louis—Louis does something I don't expect.

He pulls me backward.

Hard.

Not to scare me.

To save me.

My shoulder slams into the wall just as the tall figure takes another step out of the trees, revealing—

a face that isn't a face.

A void. A place the world forgot to finish.

And inside that emptiness, something moves.

Not eyes. Not a mouth.

Something worse. Something that never belonged to a human form at all.

Something listening.

Louis trembles violently at my back, and suddenly I know—

this is what waited for him the night he died.

And it remembers him.

And now—

it sees me.

The figure steps fully into the clearing, one long, sickening stride followed by another, like its bones were assembled incorrectly and it learned to move anyway.

Mom's voice rips out of her, raw. "Oh—Ray—Ray—get away from the windows—"

Dad is shaking so hard the chair beneath him vibrates. "Claire… don't look at it full-on. Please."

But Louis wants me to.

His warmth presses gently between my shoulder blades—not forcing, just guiding.

I turn only enough to see—

the owners.

Their faces aren't terrified.

They're calculating.

The woman stands with her coat open, hands visible, like she's approaching a nervous animal she's fed before. "Easy now," she says softly. "Storm shook you up, didn't it?"

The man steps forward too, posture careful, deliberate. "Let's not do this today, alright?" he says. "Daylight's not your time."

A cold spike punches through my stomach.

Not your time.

Dara grabs my arm, her nails digging in. "They're talking to it like it's normal."

"It's not normal," I whisper.

"No," she says. "That's the worst part."

The tall figure tilts its head toward the owners, as if weighing them against the house.

And when that empty face rotates, I feel Louis flinch against me like a terrified animal.

Dad whispers, "Claire… what is it seeing?"

I swallow. "I don't think it sees anything the way we do."

"Then what does it want?" Mae begs. "What does it want from us?"

I close my eyes—

and Louis shows me.

Not a picture. A feeling.

Cold. Tracking. Searching.

Then—

a child's panic.

Small hands pressed into dirt. Breath sharp. Heart slamming wild and uneven.

Heavy steps behind him—measured, methodical, inevitable.

I gasp and grab the table to stay upright.

"What?" Dara asks. "Claire—what did you feel?"

"He—" My voice breaks. "He fell. He fell running away from it."

Silence crashes through the room.

"He didn't die under the house," I whisper. "He crawled out. He ran. He got as far as he could."

Mom is shaking violently. "Where?" she cries. "Where did he fall?"

I open my eyes.

And suddenly—instantly—I know.

Not because of a vision.

Because Louis is pulling me toward the window, toward the trees, toward a precise gap where the snow lies differently—where the drifts dip in the exact shape a small body would make.

Frozen mid-collapse.

Buried by time.

Not forgotten.

"There," I whisper. "By the three pines. That's where he went down."

Mae collapses to the floor, sobbing. "Oh no… Claire… no…"

Dara's face goes stone-still. "I knew it. I knew that spot felt wrong."

Dad presses a shaking hand to his mouth. "All these years… I walked past that place…"

The tall figure takes another step—closer to the owners, closer to the invisible boundary between woods and yard, closer to the truth Louis is dragging into the open.

The woman lifts her hand. "That's close enough."

The man adds sharply, "You're not crossing the line."

The figure stops.

Right at the edge where something old has been waiting.

The wind dies.

The trees go still.

And the shadow turns its attention back to the house—

to me.

A low vibration presses through the walls, like the air itself is afraid.

Louis's warmth surges—stronger than ever—rushing into my chest like a child gripping my shirt.

And in that instant, I understand why he chose me.

Not just because I listen. Not just because I see. Not even because I'm intuitive.

Because it's seen this kind of seeing before.

In my blood. In someone I love.

He recognizes the same openness. The same quiet.

And he's begging me—

Don't let the tall one come for me again.

Outside, the owners finally step back, fear cracking through their practiced calm.

"He's choosing her," the woman says quietly.

The man nods, jaw tight. "Just like the last one it chose."

The last one.

Louis trembles so violently the air around me hums.

Mae screams. "THE LAST ONE?! What does that mean?!"

But the owners don't answer.

Because at that exact moment—

the tall figure lifts one long, spindly arm and points.

Not at Dad. Not at Dara. Not at the door.

At me.

Louis jerks violently in terror.

And the coldest truth settles into my bones:

The tall one didn't just hunt Louis.

It remembers him.

And now—

it knows who can see it next.

The door clicks behind the owners, and the house exhales like it's been holding its breath for hours.

No one speaks at first. Not me. Not Mae. Not Mom.

Dad sinks into the nearest chair, like his bones have finally given up pretending.

Dara moves to the window, watching the owners ' truck rattle down the lane. Her silhouette is stiff, chin tilted as if she's listening to the snow instead of the engine.

My heart hasn't slowed since the dust-smear handprint. The house remembers it too—its walls feel tight, listening.

Louis touched the window. He saw me. He chose me.

And now the house won't quiet down.

A soft tremor moves through the hallway—like a shift of weight inside the walls. Barely there. But real.

Mom flinches. "Raymond… is that him?"

Dad rubs his forehead, exhausted. "He's close."

Mae's eyes dart to me. "Claire… does he want you? Or Dad?"

I don't answer.

Because I already know.

The warmth from Louis—the strange, gentle pulse— still lingers behind my ribs like a second heartbeat. It moves in a pattern I almost recognize, as if something in me is answering back even if I don't know how.

He wants something from me.

And I want to pretend I don't feel it.

But I do.

Dara steps away from the window, slow and deliberate. "He's waiting."

"Waiting for what?" Mom snaps, her voice cracking.

Dara looks straight at me.

"For her."

My stomach drops.

Mae shakes her head. "No. No—Claire didn't do anything."

Dara tilts her head, studying me like she's reading a language only we share. Or maybe like she's searching for a weakness.

"He showed himself to you," she says. "He hasn't done that since… since before."

Her eyes flick over my face, checking for something—some old trait, some echo she's been waiting to see.

Before what?

She doesn't say.

But the way she looks at me feels like a warning wrapped in envy.

Dad lifts his head, breathing hard. "Claire… sweetheart… you don't have to—"

A soft pop comes from the hallway light.

It flickers.

Once. Twice.

Then it steadies.

Dad's breath catches. "That light's been dead since we got here. The power in this house doesn't follow wiring—never has."

Mom's hand flies to her chest. "Ray—what does that mean?"

Dara doesn't answer her.

She answers me.

"It means he's opening doors."

The warmth behind my ribs spreads—slow, steady, sure—like a hand guiding me from inside my own body.

And the house, for the first time since the storm broke, leans the way it does right before it remembers.

Not physically. Not visibly.

But leaning toward the past.

Toward the things buried beneath its floors. Toward the names it never says aloud.

Toward something deeper than snow.

Toward something he wants me to see.

A faint, unmistakable sensation travels down my spine.

Come.

I fold my arms, swallowing the fear that rises with it. "Where?"

Dara's eyes narrow.

"You already know."

And the worst part is—I do.

The pull is gentle but insistent, like a memory I've never lived. It feels older than me, older than Louis—yet threaded through my bloodline all the same.

Dad stands suddenly, wincing. "Claire, stop. Listen to me. You don't follow him alone."

"I'm not—"

But even as I speak, the warmth shifts again, drifting toward the back of the house.

Toward the woods. Toward the old foundation beyond the house. The place that existed before the ranch house. Before paint. Before names.

Dad's face drains of color. "No."

Mom shakes her head violently. "No one is going outside. No one."

But the warmth pulses again—brighter, closer—like fingers grazing mine.

Dara whispers, "He's not trying to scare her."

Mae whispers back, "Then what is he doing?"

Dara doesn't look away from me.

"He's calling her."

And the house falls into a silence that isn't silence at all.

It's expectation.

Like the house, the boy, and whatever hunts the woods are all holding the same breath.

The floorboard lifts with less resistance than I expect—like it's been waiting for someone to pull it open again.

Cold air rises up from the gap, sharp and metallic, the kind of cold that feels older than winter. The same cold that pressed against the windows when the tall one stood in the trees, listening.

Older than the house. Older than us.

Louis's warmth hovers at the edge of the opening, trembling like a candle flame fighting wind. The warmth brushes something inside me too, like a thread tugging another—a resonance   I'm not ready to name.

Behind me, someone whispers my name.

I don't turn.

If I do, I'll lose my nerve.

The crawl space yawns beneath me—black and silent, except for the faintest scrape deep inside.

Not a creature. Not an animal.

A memory shifting where it was never meant to settle.

Dad edges closer. "Claire… don't go all the way in. Just look. Just… stay where we can reach you."

Dara's voice is a low, taut thread. "She won't be alone."

She says it like a promise, but also like a warning to something else in the dark. Her eyes flick toward the outer wall, toward where the tall one stood earlier, like she knows this opening isn't just a space—it's a threshold.

I lower myself to my knees.

The cold hits first—seeping into my palms, sinking into my bones.

Then the smell.

Damp earth. Rust. Something like old metal left in the rain too long.

"He's close," I say.

Mae whimpers. "Claire, please, PLEASE don't disappear under there—I can't handle that—"

"I'm not disappearing."

My voice is steadier than I feel.

"I'm just looking."

I lean forward.

The crawl space stretches into a narrow tunnel of dirt and cracked stone, low enough that a grown man would have to belly-crawl.

But a child—a terrified, desperate child—could move quickly through it.

Dara crouches beside me. Her face is pale, eyes locked on the shadows. "This wasn't just a hiding place."

I nod.

I know.

This was an escape route. A last hope. A dead end that shouldn't have been.

Louis presses close—a warm shoulder I can't see but can feel, urgent and trembling.

Something glints at the far end of the crawl space.

Small. Metal. Like the whistle.

I inhale.

My fingers close around the small metal shape.

The whistle in my hand grows warm beating gently against my skin like a tiny, insistent pulse. It thrums faintly, almost in rhythm with Louis's presence—like whatever it meant to him, it still remembers.

Another breath rolls behind me—the tall figure's cold pressure against the outer wall, sensing movement, sensing memory. But the cold under the floor isn't the tall one—it's smaller, tighter, coiled like a trapped instinct. Different.

Louis's warmth flares sharp.

Protective. Defiant. He wants me to see. He wants me to hurry.

Dad grips the doorway. "Claire… sweetheart… what do you see?"

I swallow.

"There's something down there," I whisper. "Something he left. Something he wants me to find."

The cold deepens—not angry, but waiting.

Dara touches my shoulder.

"Then you're going to have to reach for it."

I steady my breath, take the whistle into my left hand, and extend my right toward the shadowed pit beneath the house—

And Louis's warmth floods around me like a shield, as if he's slipping ahead into the dark, guiding my hand to the place where the truth is buried.

My hand disappears into the dark before the rest of me does.

The earth is cold and loose, like something has been shifting through it for decades. Little stones press against my fingertips. A root scratches my wrist. Something metallic brushes the tip of my index finger—

Louis's warmth flares.

There.

I stretch farther, my shoulder pressing into the floorboards, my cheek almost touching the edge of the opening. The space breathes in—cold, shallow, waiting.

My fingers close around something small.

Not metal. Not stone.

Something smooth. Rounded. Warm from the dirt, but not warm like Louis.

Dad's voice shakes behind me. "Claire? Talk to me."

"I've got something," I whisper.

I pull my arm back slowly, the object clutched in my hand. Dirt falls in soft, dry cascades onto the boards as I rise.

Mom gasps. Mae covers her mouth. Dara's expression goes blank and sharp at the same time.

Because the object in my hand—

…is a marble.

The air shifts the moment I touch it—not warm like Louis, not cold like the tall figure, but something unsettled— like a tether waking up.

Clear glass, cloudy in the center, swirled with a faint streak of blue that catches the dim hallway light.

A child's marble.

Old. Scuffed.

And not Louis's.

Louis's warmth presses against my back, urgent, insisting.

Dad steps forward, knees shaking. "Oh Gosh…"

Mom whispers, "Raymond… is that—?"

Dad nods once, voice breaking.

"That's the other boy's."

The room tilts.

My breath goes thin.

The marble sits in my palm like a heartbeat from a decade no one ever spoke about.

From a boy Dara barely remembers. From a boy Pawpaw swore wasn't real. From a boy we were never allowed to ask about.

Dara's jaw clenches. She swallows hard, looking at anything but the marble.

Mae's voice is tiny. "Are you saying... there were two?"

Dad lowers himself into a crouch beside me, struck as though he's staring at a ghost with weight.

"There was Louis," he whispers, "and years later... there was another one."

Mom starts shaking. "Raymond, stop. PLEASE stop. We said we wouldn't—"

But Dad shakes his head.

"He died on this land too, Lillian."

The hallway seems to freeze.

Not silent—listening.

Louis's warmth tightens around my ribs, not jealous, not frightened—

Warning.

Dara takes a step back from the crawl-space opening. "He's showing her where the second one went."

Mom stumbles into a chair. "Why now? Why BOTH now?"

I stare at the marble.

Louis trembles beside me. Not grief—fear. Not for himself, but for what else was buried here.

Because he's afraid—

for the second boy.

Because the tall figure in the woods…

…never belonged to Louis.

A cold understanding snakes through my spine.

I look at Dad, Mae, Dara—then at the marble—then at the trembling warmth pressed against my shoulder.

And I whisper the truth:

"Louis isn't connected to the thing outside at all. The other boy is. That's why Louis is shaking. The tall one didn't hunt Louis—it watched him. But the other boy was taken—or changed into something that couldn't come back."

Dad's face folds. "No…"

Dara whispers, "It never was Louis."

Mae starts crying. "Then—then what is it?"

The whistle in my left hand burns suddenly hot.

Louis's warmth withdraws from my side like a child stepping behind a parent's leg.

A coldness leaks under the floorboards—not him, but what follows him.

The tall figure is moving closer.

The marble in my palm pulses—or maybe my hand is shaking—

—and the house, for the first time since we arrived, feels like something underneath it is waking up.

Louis's whisper brushes my ear again.

Not *hurry* this time.

But a new word.

A name.

"…Tommy."

"…Tommy."

His name hangs in the air like frost—suspended, fragile, waiting to shatter at the slightest breath.

Dad closes his eyes, pain folding across his face in a way I've never seen. Mom reaches for him instinctively, but he doesn't look at her. He just stares at the crawl space like a boy Ray once was is staring back.

Mae whispers, terrified, "Tommy? You mean—the drowning boy? The one from the old story?"

Louis presses against my back, trembling so hard I feel it through my spine.

Dad nods once. "Yes. Tommy."

"But that was just a rumor," Mae says, voice pitching higher. "A stupid legend people told about the creek—"

"No," Dad croaks. "It wasn't a legend."

Mom flinches like she's been struck. "Raymond— stop—PLEASE—"

Louis's warmth turns sharp with urgency.

He needs me to understand what I'm holding. He needs me to hear the truth he couldn't speak when he was alive.

I tighten my grip around the marble.

A vibration rolls through the floorboards—deep and slow, like something wet dragging itself through dirt.

Dara stiffens instantly. "Claire. Back up."

I don't.

I can't.

Because Louis isn't pulling me away this time.

He's standing his ground.

Dad's voice shakes. "Tommy didn't drown, Claire."

The house seems to freeze around the words.

Shutters groan. Pipes click. The lights dim for a long, uneasy moment.

Mom gasps, "Raymond, DON'T—"

"He ran," Dad says, louder now. "He hid. And he tried to crawl under this house—just like Louis."

A sick, cold heaviness blooms under the floorboards, pressing upward like a tide.

Mae backs into the wall, hands covering her mouth. "Claire—Claire—something's under us—"

Something moves beneath me.

Not fast. Not frantic. Purposeful.

The boards rise a fraction of an inch.

Louis's warmth slams into me, shielding, bracing, desperate.

Because what's coming isn't him.

Dara's voice drops to a whisper almost too thin to hear. "It's not Louis."

I swallow hard. "It's Tommy… isn't it?"

The whistle in my other hand heats so suddenly I nearly drop it.

The answer doesn't come from anyone in the room.

It comes from beneath us.

A voice.

Wet. Warped. Like a boy who never got his last breath above water.

Long vowels stretched beyond human.

Like something that tried to scream underwater and never recovered.

"…Claire…"

Mom's knees buckle. Mae starts sobbing openly. Dad looks like he's about to pass out.

Dara's eyes go wide, but she doesn't move—she won't leave my side, even with that… thing… calling my name.

The floorboards bulge again.

"…Claire… come…"

It's not a request.

It's a summoning.

Louis's warmth flares—a shield, a barrier, a scream without sound.

He's terrified.

Terrified for me. Terrified of Tommy.

Dara grabs the edge of the wall to steady herself. "Claire—listen to me. Whatever you hear—whatever he sounds like—that is NOT a little boy."

I whisper, "What is he then?"

A long silence.

Then Dara answers.

Not with softness. Not with caution.

With truth.

"He's what you become when you die afraid… and no one comes."

Her voice cracks—not because she doubts it, but because she's seen pieces of this before.

The floor beneath me thunders once, a heavy blow that rattles dishes in the kitchen.

Mom screams. Mae pulls Dad away from the opening.

Louis presses into my back—a warm, small body trying to hold off a tidal wave.

I raise the marble into the scant hallway light.

It pulses faintly.

Blue-white. Alive. Calling.

Not to me.

To him.

Another dragging sound, this one closer—too close—right beneath the thin wood between my feet and the earth.

Louis whispers again—this time not a name, not a plea:

"...don't..."

My breath shakes.

But I stay where I am.

Because the truth isn't finished yet.

And neither is Tommy.

The boards beneath me inhale shallowly, like something under the house is gathering breath for the first time in decades—

not to live.

To be heard.

CHAPTER THIRTY-FOUR — THE PATH BACK

The floor settles after Tommy's voice fades, but the air in the hallway doesn't move. It hangs there—thick, cold, waiting—as if the house itself is bracing for what comes next.

Louis presses closer to my back, his warmth tightening like a frightened child gripping the hem of a coat. He isn't urging me forward anymore. He's holding on.

For a moment, no one speaks.

Mae is still crying quietly, shoulders shaking. Mom has both hands clamped over her ears, like Tommy's voice is something she can still hear—something she's trying to shove out of her skull. Dad keeps staring at the crawl gap, jaw clenched, ashamed of whatever he buried, whatever he let stay buried.

Only Dara stands still.

Unblinking. Listening.

Her eyes flick toward the window—toward the woods—then toward the far side of the property, where the old Civil War house sits heavy and rotting behind the hedgerow. The memory of it crosses her face in a single tightening of her mouth.

I see it. I feel it.

And then I remember—

The three of us in that doorway—it feels like hours ago. Gray light. Dust suspended in still air.

Dara's voice echoing through the empty front room:

"He used to perform here… Tommy. He liked pretending he had an audience."

It felt strange then. Now it feels like a warning we didn't know how to hear.

The unease returns—quiet, tilting—the same sensation I had on the road our first night here, when something stepped into the headlights and Dad called it a deer.

A prickling starts down my spine—Louis's fear sharpening into direction. A pull. Not toward the crawl gap this time.

Toward the land.

The path across the back acreage drops into my awareness all at once, like a memory I've never owned:

The slope behind the barn. The break in the fence line. The trail that leads toward the old Civil War house.

Louis is showing me.

Not in words. Not in images.

In instinct.

"Claire?" Dad says softly. "Where's he leading you now?"

I swallow. "He doesn't want me down there," I whisper, eyes on the gap. "Not with Tommy."

A tremble of agreement moves through Louis, brushing my ribs with warmth.

"But he wants me somewhere else."

Mom's head snaps up. "Absolutely not—absolutely not—after what we just heard, no one is going outside—"

Her voice dies on the last word.

Because something shifts outside the window.

Not a shadow. Not a figure.

A weight.

The tall one.

Not at the woods now—nearer.

The house seems to brace.

Mae shakes her head, tears bright again. "Claire… please don't say what I think you're going to say."

I don't look at her.

I can't.

Louis's warmth moves again—insistent. Away from the crawl gap. Away from Tommy. Toward the path. Toward the old Civil War house—toward the first place Tommy learned what was following him.

I whisper, barely able to shape it: "He wants me to go back… to where Tommy started."

Louis tugs again—small, urgent, unmistakable—and for the first time, I feel the direction not in my spine—

but in my feet.

Sound dips for a second, like the house just swallowed the world.

My toes angle toward the mudroom door.

Toward boots. Coats. The back acreage.

The Civil War house feels like a memory breathing through a cracked window—cold, old, waiting.

The land bends every thought toward it, the way it did in my dreams before we came back.

Dad hears it in me before I move. "Claire. Don't."

His voice cracks, older than it's ever sounded. "We don't know what's out there."

Dara's jaw tightens. "We know what's out there," she murmurs, eyes narrowing toward the wall where that pressure pressed minutes ago.

And she's right.

We do.

But Louis isn't trying to lead me into danger.

He's trying to lead me around it.

The whistle warms in my palm, then cools—like he's speaking through temperature. A flicker of understanding travels up my arm.

"He wants us to go now," I whisper.

Mae chokes on a sob. "Claire—I—I can't lose you, too. Mom's losing it. Dad's barely standing. And Dara—"

She stops because Dara's face is unreadable—carved into something between dread and clarity.

Dara steps closer to me—closer than she has since childhood. "If she's going out there," she says, "she's not going alone."

Mom shakes her head violently. "No. No, I won't let it happen again. I won't lose another—"

She bites the words back so hard she winces.

I freeze.

Again.

The quiet that settles isn't calm.

It's the kind that realizes we've all been holding different parts of the same secret.

Dara answers first.

Soft. Bitter. Tired. "We already did lose someone. Long before this storm."

Dad flinches. So does Mom.

Mae wipes her eyes, confused. "What are you talking about?"

The room tightens.

Louis presses into my back—steadying me, grounding me, bracing me for something I didn't know I was supposed to hear.

Dara looks at me.

Just me.

"You don't know?" she whispers.

My throat closes. "Know what?"

Dara takes a long breath, her gaze flicking once—just once—toward the Civil War house, as if the land itself is listening.

"Tommy wasn't the only one who died on this property."

A sharp cold slides down my spine.

Louis goes still.

Dad shifts like he can block the words with his body, but Dara keeps going.

"He wasn't even the last."

The lights flicker once—hard—rattling the glass in the windows.

Dad whispers, begging, "Dara, please don't."

But she ignores him.

Because she isn't talking for him.

She's talking for me.

"For Claire to understand why Louis chose her," Dara says. "Why he trusts her. Why he's pulling her now."

Mom grabs the counter to steady herself. "Dara—stop—stop—"

But it's too late.

Dara steps closer, voice so low only I and whatever listens beneath the floorboards can hear. "Because you're the only one who can walk onto that land without something following you," she says. "Without feeding it."

Mom collapses into a chair.

Mae goes pale.

Dad closes his eyes.

And Louis trembles—

not with fear.

With relief.

Like he's been waiting for someone to finally say it out loud.

Dara inhales. "If you go, we go with you. But if you stay…"

Her voice catches for the first time.

"…he'll never stop calling."

I don't answer.

I can't.

Because the answer is already forming inside me— pulsing through the whistle, tugging my ribs toward the back door, pressing my feet toward the land that shaped everything that broke us.

The Civil War house is waiting.

And so is the truth.

The whistle warms once—firm, final.

A signal. A direction.

Dad sees my shoulders shift toward the mudroom. "Wait. Claire—wait."

His voice is thin. "If you go out there now, you might not find your way back."

Louis presses in gently.

A reassurance.

Dara watches me with a strange, steady calm—like she's finally accepted something she fought for years. "If she waits," Dara says, "the tall one will get ahead of her."

Mom lets out a soft, broken sound. "Why is this happening?"

Mae takes her hand. I don't think she has the strength for words anymore.

Louis tugs again—gentle but urgent.

Now.

I nod once.

It isn't an announcement. It isn't bravery.

"We go," I say quietly.

Mom gasps. Dad stiffens. Mae shakes her head once—but she doesn't tell me no.

Only Dara steps toward me without hesitation.

"I'm with you."

Dad swallows. "You shouldn't be. You don't have to—"

Dara cuts him off, voice razor-thin. "I'm not losing Claire too."

The *too* isn't explained. It doesn't need to be.

Louis flares—approval.

I pull on my boots.

Dara does the same.

Mae hovers near us, shaking. "I should stay with Mom and Dad," she whispers—already drifting closer to the doorway.

Louis urges me toward the door again.

I grip the knob.

The metal is freezing—so cold it almost burns.

The moment I crack it open, the air hits me:

Not winter-cold.

Earth-cold.

Grave-cold.

A warning and a welcome at the same time.

Dara falls in behind me, steps careful, controlled. "Where's he leading you?"

I don't answer with words.

I lift the whistle.

It warms—pointing right.

Toward the old path. Toward the abandoned Civil War house sitting like rot among the trees.

Mom calls out once, voice splitting. "Claire—"

I turn just enough to meet her eyes.

"I'll come back."

She shakes her head, tears slipping down her face. "That's what we said… with Tommy."

Dad flinches so hard he turns away.

Louis presses around me—steady, protective.

I step outside.

The door closes behind us with a soft click, shutting in the thin warmth of the house and swallowing the voices of my family.

The world outside is white and silent.

But the path to the Civil War house isn't.

It breathes.

Waiting.

Each step forward feels less like walking and more like stepping into someone else's unfinished story.

The snow under our boots isn't soft anymore.

It's crusted—brittle—like ice over something that refused to settle.

Dara walks half a step behind me, eyes scanning the tree line. She doesn't talk, and I don't ask her to. The quiet between us isn't distance anymore.

It's survival.

Louis moves with us—warm pulses at my back—guiding my steps with a precision that feels like memory stitched into instinct.

Every few feet, he tugs—

left. slower. stop.

Dara notices. "He's… blocking a path."

I nod. "He doesn't want us stepping somewhere."

Her breath hitches. "Where Tommy—"

"We keep going," I say, and she doesn't finish.

The farther we get from the house, the more the woods feel… aware.

Branches tilt just enough to attend, holding their snow like held breath.

The silence isn't empty.

It's listening.

Old fence posts lean inward. The path curves where it didn't used to—

—or maybe it always curved, and the land just hid it.

Louis tightens suddenly and pulls hard.

"Stop," I say.

Dara freezes instantly.

We're at the edge of a small clearing.

The Civil War house is still a hundred yards away, but I feel its presence like breath on my neck.

And right in front of us—barely visible beneath fresh snow—is a long, dark indentation in the ground.

A collapsed place. Soft earth underneath.

Dara whispers, "Claire…?"

Louis presses into my spine—terrified, insistent.

We don't step forward.

Not an inch.

Because underneath that snow—

Tommy crawled.

And didn't get out.

Dara covers her mouth. "Oh gosh."

The wind shifts then—

a cold, unnatural sweep from the right.

Dara grabs my arm, nails digging in. "Did you see that?"

I did.

A tall shadow—too thin, too long—slides behind the line of gray pines.

Not approaching.

Positioning. Watching. Waiting.

Louis flares hot—protective, trembling.

Dara whispers through her teeth, "He's keeping the tall one off you."

"But he's terrified," I murmur.

"Of that thing? Wouldn't you be?"

Louis tugs again—firm—leading us around the collapsed ground in a wide arc.

We follow.

My breath fogs in sharp bursts.

Dara steps closer, shoulder brushing mine. "Claire… I don't remember everything about Tommy. I know I said things earlier, at the old house, but some of that—"

Her voice breaks off.

She's remembering.

But not fully.

And not safely.

Louis slows—gentle now—then steadies me before a root.

We're almost to the Civil War house clearing.

I feel it.

Old air. Older secrets.

Walls that have held more than history.

The house is just beyond the bruise-colored trees, its roofline barely visible through the branches.

Louis stops us again.

Not out of fear.

Out of readiness.

The truth is close.

And Tommy is closer.

Dara's breath comes out in a thin, shaking thread. "Claire… whatever happened in there… I think we're about to walk back into it."

I tighten my grip on the whistle.

Louis wraps around me like small hands bracing themselves.

We take one more step toward the house—

—when the snow just ahead sinks inward, as if something unseen has just knelt there.

The impression is child-height.

Kneeling.

Fresh.

Dara grips my sleeve. "Claire… don't step toward it."

Louis tightens around my ribs—not fearfully.

Warning.

He marks places where we'll be safe, and where we won't.

I shift a hair to the left.

The warmth eases.

Dara exhales shakily. "How does he know after all these years…?"

I don't answer.

Because the truth pulses through my palm where the whistle rests:

He never stopped walking this land.

The Civil War house breaks fully into view—

gray boards, bowed porch, windows black as missing eyes.

A place built for shelter, then used for the opposite.

Louis presses in again—gentler. He wants us closer.

Dara hesitates at the tree line. "Claire… before we go in, you need to know… some of what I said last time we came here—about Tommy—"

She stops. Her throat tightens.

I wait.

I can feel her remembering—and fighting something that doesn't want her to.

Dara swallows hard. "When we were here before… I said he liked to perform in this house. That he used to sing. That he did little shows."

I nod.

She shakes her head slowly. "Those weren't my memories."

She looks at me—

truly looks—

and I feel Louis go rigid beside us.

"I didn't remember that on my own," Dara whispers. "Someone showed me."

Louis snaps hot—

not at Dara.

At the house. At the thing inside it.

A long crack runs down one of the porch posts— sharp enough that I flinch back.

Dara gasps. "What was that?"

Louis huddles closer, trembling, pushing us forward and bracing us all at once.

Behind us, that tall pressure shifts deeper among the trees—not approaching, but circling.

Dara whispers, "He's trapping it."

The Civil War house looms ahead—

half-sunk, half-standing—

a mouth waiting to swallow what's left of the truth.

Louis leads us to the porch steps.

Each one groans under our weight,

like the wood remembers the shape of small hands.

A shiver climbs my spine.

Dara stops on the second step, voice barely a breath. "I think… the last time Tommy was alive… it was here."

Louis answers—soft, grief-sick—beneath my ribs.

The front door isn't locked.

It's swollen from age, pushed open by storms and time and something trying to leave—or trying to get back inside.

I put my hand on the knob.

It's cold.

Not house-cold.

The silence changes shape.

Dara stands right beside me now—solid, ready. "Claire… whatever's in there… Louis wants us to see it."

Louis presses into my spine—

a child hiding behind me, begging without words: Please see.

I brace myself.

The wind stills. That tall presence stops moving.

The house seems to inhale.

And I push the door open.

The front room smells like cold earth and shut-in years.

The boards bow under our weight, not from rot but from memory. This place held too much for too long.

Dara steps in first, her breath clouding.

I follow.

Mae lingers in the doorway, shaking.

Louis hovers behind me—he won't cross the threshold. Not here. Not in this building.

That's the first sign something is different.

I whisper, "Why won't he come in?"

Dara answers without looking back. "Because this isn't his death place."

And maybe because whatever claimed Tommy still thinks this house belongs to it.

The words settle in the cold like dust.

I take a few steps deeper. The walls are the same gray planks I remember from childhood, but the shadows feel heavier now, like they've been waiting for someone who can feel them.

Mae wraps her arms tight around her ribs. "I hate how this place feels."

Dara doesn't turn. She points to the back staircase—the narrow one with the broken banister.

"That's where Tommy fell," she says quietly.

Mae flinches. "Dara, please—"

But Dara shakes her head.

She isn't telling a story.

She's following a memory her mind tried to bury.

"I never believed Papa about the drowning," Dara whispers. "Not even when I was little."

The air tightens.

Mae looks up slowly. "Why didn't you say something?"

"Because Papa told me not to."

There it is.

A fracture in the narrative we grew up with.

A crack in the story Papa repeated for forty years.

I step closer. "Dara… what did he say?"

Dara exhales, breath shivering out of her.

"He said if anyone asked, Tommy drowned in the lake. And if I repeated what I saw, people would think something was wrong with me."

Mae's breath catches.

I whisper, "What did you see?"

Dara swallows hard, eyes fixed on the staircase like she's watching it happen again.

"I saw Tommy run out of this house," she says softly. "I saw him fall down the steps. I heard him scream—"

Her jaw trembles.

"—and I saw the tall thing behind him."

A cold pressure shifts through the room—soundless, absolute.

Mae clamps her hands over her ears. "No—Dara, stop—"

But Dara shakes her head, tears gathering.

"I told Papa," she whispers. "I told him what was chasing Tommy. And Papa grabbed me and said, 'You didn't see anything. Nothing followed him. Nothing lives in those woods.'"

My chest tightens. "He was protecting you."

"No," Dara says.

Her voice is small. Torn open. True.

"He was protecting himself."

The house answers with a low groan, like something beneath the floor remembers her words.

I step closer. "From what?"

Dara looks at me—really looks—and her expression folds.

"From the truth."

A gust of cold hits the side of the house.

Not weather.

Recognition.

Something outside knows we're speaking its name without speaking it.

Louis flares behind me—small, frantic, protective—but he still won't enter.

Dara's eyes drift toward the back corner of the house—the place where the old coal stove used to sit.

"That's where Papa found him," she whispers.

"Found who?" Mae cries. "Tommy? The tall thing—what?"

Dara's answer is barely breath. "Papa found Tommy hiding in the corner."

"And he was alive."

I freeze.

Mae's knees nearly buckle. "Alive? Then why—why did Papa—"

Dara closes her eyes.

"Papa tried to bring him home," she says. "Tommy was confused… terrified… like he didn't recognize anything. Papa thought getting him out of this house would help."

She swallows hard.

"He carried Tommy toward the lake path because the trail was clearest in the dark. He said Tommy wriggled free and ran."

Mae sobs. "Then—then what happened?"

Dara wipes her cheek.

"Papa chased him," she whispers. "He chased him until he couldn't see his own hands. But Tommy disappeared somewhere near the water. They found his shoe by the lake the next morning… and Papa said the rest was taken by the night."

My breath leaves me.

Mae makes a sound like a scream swallowed whole.

Louis trembles so violently the air shivers.

And I understand, all at once, why Louis shook when Tommy got close.

Why that tall presence knows Papa's bloodline.

Why the land chose me.

Because the truth doesn't belong to Louis.

It belongs to Tommy.

And he isn't done.

Outside, something tall shifts beside the window—its silhouette stretching across the wall like a stain.

Dara whispers, "Claire... he followed us here."

The window hisses—glass tightening as if touched by cold fingers.

A long scrape drags across the siding.

Not claws. Not branches.

Something reaching.

Mae clamps her hands over her mouth to keep from screaming.

Louis crashes into me from the doorway like a small, terrified body trying to hide behind me. He trembles so hard it raises the hairs on my arms.

Dara whispers, "Don't move."

But the thing outside already knows where we are.

It leans.

The fog on the glass blooms in a single breath.

Louis presses harder against me. He isn't leading me now.

He's shielding me.

Dara steps beside me, shoulders squared even though she's shaking. "Claire... listen to me. Tommy doesn't want you. He wants what you carry."

I swallow. "The marble?"

"No," Dara whispers. "The truth."

A low hum vibrates through the floorboards, climbs the walls.

Mae backs into the doorway. "We should go. We need to go—Dara, please—"

But Dara doesn't move.

Her eyes stay fixed on the window, where that silhouette leans closer, listening through the glass.

Then she says something that turns my stomach to ice:

"He thinks you can undo him."

The front door slams hard enough that dust shakes loose from the beams.

Louis whimpers—not out loud, but inside the warmth around me. A plea. A warning.

Dara grabs my arm. "Claire. Stay with me. Stay here."

But Louis pulls—not forward, not away—backward.

Toward the hallway.

Toward the room Papa refused to speak of.

Toward the place where Tommy hid after the fall.

Mae sobs, "He wants her alone—why does he want her alone—"

"He doesn't," Dara says, choking back fear. "He wants her away from Tommy."

And that's when I understand:

Louis isn't hiding from the tall figure.

He's trying to lead me away from it.

The warmth surges behind me, desperate.

I take a step back.

Dara follows.

Mae stumbles after us.

Outside, the silhouette jerks—

a long, unnatural movement like a puppet yanked on a string.

Something slams the wall.

The boards shudder.

The window fogs over again.

Louis flares, begging:

Go. Now.

"Move," Dara snaps, grabbing Mae by the sleeve.

We hurry into the back hallway—the place where the shadows bend differently and the air feels heavier, like it remembers every handprint, every held breath, every plea that went unanswered.

The tall thing drags along the siding, scraping, following.

Not fast.

Relentless.

Dara rounds the corner first. "Claire—hurry—"

But as I reach the hall, something stops me cold.

The shadows shift.

Not like darkness.

Like someone small is stepping into place.

Louis stands in front of me—not visible, but unmistakably there—a warm blockade between me and whatever is trying to enter from the other side.

He's shaking.

He's scared.

But he's standing.

For me.

Dara whispers, awed and afraid, "Claire… he's been waiting for you to come here."

Louis presses his warmth against my hand—not pulling this time.

Pointing.

At a door we haven't opened yet.

At a room Papa refused to speak of.

At the place where Tommy hid after the fall.

Outside, something slams the house again—harder, angrier, closer.

But Louis stays planted between us like a child refusing to let a monster through.

And something inside me—something inherited—knows what he wants.

The same part of me that has always stilled a room without trying, that knows when to go quiet before anyone speaks.

I tighten my grip on the marble.

"Okay," I whisper. "Show me."

Louis nudges the door.

And the handle starts to turn.

The doorknob turns under its own weight—slow, deliberate, like someone on the other side is matching the pressure of my fingertips.

Louis's warmth presses into my spine, not guiding this time.

Steadying.

The air around my skin dips for a moment—the same subtle hush I've felt before I quiet a room without meaning to.

Dara stands to my right, breath tight, shoulders squared. Behind us, Mae lingers at the hall entrance, torn between fear and the need to see.

The door creaks open.

Cold spills out—different from the rest of the house.

Not lake-cold. Not winter-cold.

Something else.

A cold that feels *familiar* in the wrong way. Like the tall one has been near it before. Like it seeped in and never left.

The room is small.

Dust-sick.

Shadows pulled tight against the walls.

Nothing moves.

But the air is held—too still, like a throat refusing to swallow.

Louis nudges once—gentle, apologetic—like he wishes he could walk in beside me, but the doorway pushes back.

Dara whispers, "Claire... what do you feel?"

I'm not sure at first.

Then it comes.

Not a pull. Not fear.

Something deeper.

Recognition.

"I've been here," I breathe.

Not from memory.

From blood.

Dara's head snaps toward me. "What? No—you haven't—"

But she stops.

Because she sees the way Louis steadies me.

The way the air around me quiets.

The way the room presses in, almost—relieved.

Dara swallows. "He showed you this place before."

I step inside.

The boards groan under my boots—long, low creaks like old bones shifting in sleep.

The smell is different from the rest of the house.

Earth. Paper.

Something metallic and faded—like iron left too long in damp.

Dara follows one step behind me.

Mae stays in the doorway, shaking so hard the frame answers her. "Claire—don't go too far—please—just... don't."

I don't answer.

Because the shadows in the back corner shift.

Not movement.

Memory.

Louis pulses behind me— faint but steady—rapid, frightened, pleading.

He doesn't want me near the corner.

But the corner is where the truth is.

A shape begins to resolve in the dim—low to the ground.

Not a person.

Not a monster.

A remnant. A thing left behind.

The air thickens.

Dara whispers, "Claire… what do you see?"

I crouch slowly.

The dark resolves into an object—

a small wooden box.

Warped at the edges.

Lid cracked.

Carved with initials worn nearly to nothing.

My fingertips hover over it.

Louis presses in—

Don't.

Not yet.

Beside the box, the floorboards dip slightly—an impression, child-sized. Like knees had lived there.

Dara sees it and clamps a hand over her mouth.

"Oh—no."

Louis trembles so hard I feel it in my ribs.

This is where Tommy waited.

This is where he tried to stay small enough to vanish.

The house tightens around us—boards shifting, a slow complaint traveling up the studs—as if the building is bracing.

Dara kneels beside me, voice stripped down to a thread. "Claire… if you open that box… everything changes."

I nod.

Because I know.

This is the last thing Papa starved with silence.

The last thing Louis couldn't show me alone.

I set my hand on the lid.

Louis draws close—so close it feels like he's holding my forearm.

Not stopping me.

Steadying me.

Ready.

I lift the lid.

It opens with a soft, splintered sigh—like it has been waiting decades to be found and dreading it the whole time.

Inside, layered carefully—placed by small hands that didn't trust the world—are only three objects.

Nothing dramatic.

Nothing that screams.

Just quiet things.

Quiet things that weigh more than bone.

Dara leans closer, holding herself still.

Mae grips the doorframe hard enough her knuckles bleach.

Louis wraps around my shoulders.

Bracing.

First—fabric.

A strip of faded blue cotton, frayed, edges torn clean.

Small enough to have belonged to a child's shirt.

Dara makes a sound I feel more than hear. "I remember that. Tommy wore blue every day. Papa said it kept him from getting lost."

My stomach twists.

I lift the fabric with two fingers—gently, reverently.

It's soft in the way only children's things ever are.

Underneath it—

Second—a hinge.

A tiny rusted hinge.

Bent.

Detached from anything.

I frown.

A hinge—why would a child hide—

Dara goes still.

Her hand flies to her mouth.

"Claire."

She points past me to the narrow staircase—the broken banister.

"The railing," she whispers. "The one he grabbed when he ran. Papa said it broke."

The hinge.

From the fall.

From the moment everything tipped.

Louis trembles—gentle, grieving—like the house is pressing a thumb into an old bruise.

And beneath those two objects—

Third—a folded paper.

A square of paper darkened at the edges by damp and time.

The fold is crooked, hurried—made by a hand that didn't have the luxury of calm.

My chest tightens.

Dara whispers, "Claire… don't—"

But I already know I have to.

I pick it up.

The paper is cold—the kind of cold that holds onto fear.

I unfold it carefully.

Inside is a child's drawing.

A stick figure house—crooked.

A stick figure boy—smaller.

A stick figure shadow—taller than the house.

And behind the boy—

a circle.

Not neat.

Not playful.

Pressed over and over, so hard the paper nearly tore.

A ring around the boy.

A ring around the smallness of him.

A ring meant to hold.

The room tilts, just slightly—not from dizziness.

From meaning.

Dara whispers, "What is that?"

Louis presses into my back—urgent, shaking.

"It's where he tried to stay safe," I breathe. "Where he thought it couldn't reach."

Mae's voice breaks in the doorway. "But it did, Claire. It did."

I run my thumb over the circle, trying to feel what he felt.

Louis leans into me harder—a silent plea.

Dara leans close, voice thin. "Claire… look at the bottom corner."

I pull the drawing closer to the dim windowlight.

In the lower right, scratched in uneven letters—

C-L-A-I-R

Not neat. Not sure. Like the hand stopped mid-name.

Dara's breath leaves her.

"Claire… he wrote your name."

The boards beneath us moan as if they're shifting under invisible weight.

Mae whispers, horrified, "How? How would Tommy know Claire? She was barely more than a baby!"

Louis jolts against my ribs—a sharp pulse.

Not fear.

Recognition.

Dara's eyes widen. "He didn't mean *you*. Not exactly. He meant the line."

A name passed like a warning.

The drawing trembles in my hand—not from movement.

From the fact of it.

"He was trying to warn whoever came next," Dara whispers. "Whoever had the gift. Whoever would hear him."

My pulse hammers.

Louis presses into my palms, into my arms, into my ribs—steadying me for what my mind doesn't want to name yet.

Because the message wasn't for Tommy.

Wasn't for Papa.

Wasn't for Dara.

It was for the next Claire who would come back to this land and listen.

And that person is me.

A cold roll moves through the room then—slow, creeping, deliberate.

Dara goes rigid.

Mae clamps both hands over her mouth.

Because from the corner where Tommy once hid—

a shape begins to gather.

Not fully.

Not clearly.

Just the impression of a crouched child.

The air buckles around it, rippling like heat—only colder.

And beside it—

a taller bend of shadow.

Louis surges, desperate.

Dara grabs my wrist. "Claire—whatever you do—don't move toward it—"

But the shadow straightens.

And the circle on the paper deepens beneath my fingers—darkening as if someone is pressing charcoal from the other side of the page.

Something inside me settles.

Not fear.

Not force.

The Quiet—familiar as muscle memory—slides into place behind my ribs.

The room listens.

The shadow inhales.

And I understand, cold and certain:

the house remembers us—
and it remembers *what we fed it.*

CHAPTER THIRTY-SIX—THE HOUSE SPEAKS

The circle on the paper darkens again—not from my touch, not from light, but from something unseen pressing into the memory of the page.

The air tightens.

Not violently.

Attentive.

Dara drags in a shaky breath. "Claire—stop looking at it—put it down—"

"I can't," I whisper. Not because I'm trapped—but because something has finally settled.

Louis's warmth has gone still against my shoulders. Not pulling. Not warning.

Holding me in place.

Balanced.

In the far corner, the small crouched shape twitches—a sharp jerk, like knees shifting on old wood.

Mae makes a strangled sound and stumbles back. "Claire, please—let's go—let's just go—"

Dara grabs her arm, eyes locked on the corner. "No one moves."

The shadow rises another inch.

Then another.

Not fluid.

Not human.

The room temperature drops—not winter-cold, but the kind that steals breath from lungs that aren't ours.

Louis presses into my spine, trembling so hard my teeth click.

I center myself.

Not panic. Not force.

One steady breath.

The way the Quiet moves through me when I don't *use* it—when I let it align.

The way I've stilled rooms before words arrived.

Dara sees it.

Her eyes snap to me. "Claire," she whispers, "you're Quieting."

I don't answer.

The air around me thickens—not with fear, but with precision.

The paper in my hand vibrates.

The circle bleeds darker.

And the crouched figure sharpens—a small curled spine, thin shoulders hunched forward, hands pressed over ears.

A boy trying not to hear.

Trying not to be seen.

Tommy.

My throat tightens.

"Tommy," I whisper.

The shadow flinches.

His head jerks upward at a wrong, painful angle.

Mae lets out a broken cry and sinks to the floor.

Dara steps in front of her without looking away. "Don't speak to him unless you're sure he's listening."

But he is.

I feel it.

Louis feels it.

Louis's warmth presses into my ribs—*hold the line*.

The taller shadow behind Tommy stretches, long arms climbing the wall, head tilting toward us.

Dara mutters, low and furious, "It's keeping him here. It's using him."

I step forward—slow, deliberate.

Louis braces me. Not stopping.

Steadying.

The Quiet sharpens—not power, not dominance.

Clarity.

The ability to separate signal from noise.

I let a measured breath pass through my nose.

The temperature shifts by a hair.

The tall figure freezes.

Dara grips my arm. "Claire—what did you just do?"

Tommy lifts his head.

His eyes—

No whites. No pupils.

Just pale, waterwashed gray.

Dara gasps. "Don't look at him—"

But Tommy isn't looking at me.

He's looking at the drawing.

At the circle.

At the name scratched by a child who didn't know who would come next.

His mouth moves.

Barely sound.

"Safe."

The Quiet tightens—coiling around my breath like a second pulse.

The tall figure spasms, limbs jerking like a marionette pulled too hard.

Dara pulls me back, but I hold my ground.

"No. He's not attacking," I say quietly. "He's reacting."

"To what?" she snaps.

"The Quiet."

Louis presses close—warm, terrified—but he doesn't pull me away.

He braces *with* me.

The tall shadow recoils from the center of the room—from the circle etched into memory, from the boy inside it.

Tommy shifts.

And then—

He stands.

Not fully.

Not cleanly.

But enough.

His shoulders are wrong. His arms too thin. His head tilted in the posture of someone who never healed correctly.

Still a child.

A broken one.

"Tommy," I say softly. "I'm listening."

The tall figure slams into the wall—*hard*—wood cracking.

Dara snaps, "Claire—stop—"

But Tommy lifts one trembling hand.

Points to me.

Then to the circle.

Then—slowly, with effort that costs him—he points toward the door at the far back of the house.

The room Papa never allowed anyone to enter.

Louis's warmth cools—not cold.

Solemn.

A plea.

Dara whispers, "He wants you to finish what he couldn't say."

Tommy's mouth opens.

What comes out isn't a word.

It's direction.

I don't step forward.

I don't step back.

I Quiet.

One breath in.

One breath out.

The room stills.

The tall figure locks in place—arms stretched, head cocked, listening for permission that never comes.

Tommy's finger stays raised.

Pointing.

The truth isn't in the corner.

It's behind that door.

Dara steps beside me, voice shaking but firm. "Claire… you don't have to go in there alone."

"No," I whisper. "I think I do."

The Quiet settles—not sharp now, but deep.

Grounded.

Mae sobs softly in the hall. "Claire—please—don't leave us—"

"I'm not leaving," I say. "I'm going forward."

Tommy flickers—not calling, not begging.

Guiding.

Dara grips the doorframe as I pass. "If anything shifts—say my name. Out loud."

I nod.

Louis moves with me, warmth radiating through my spine, bracing every step.

The tall figure twitches but does not advance.

Something holds it.

Or someone.

I place my hand on the knob of the back room.

It isn't cold.

It resists.

Like the door doesn't want to remember.

Dara whispers behind me, "Is Louis okay?"

"He's… trying."

The warmth presses—steady, steady, don't stop—

The handle clicks.

The door opens.

Darkness spills out.

Not empty.

Waiting.

The smell comes first.

Old soil. Wet wood. Time.

Air thick as a sealed room that never wanted light.

Louis hesitates at the threshold.

The threshold resists him.

My chest tightens.

"Why?"

The room answers.

Not Tommy.

Not Louis.

The room itself.

"…because this is mine."
Dara gasps. "Who—who said that?"
The voice isn't a boy's.
Not the tall thing.
Older.
Dry.
Breaking.
Familiar enough to hurt.
I lift the whistle.
It warms instantly.
Louis presses into me once—*go, but go carefully.*
I step inside.
The floor dips—earth disturbed long ago.
Dara stays at the doorway.
She wants to follow.
Something warns her back.
Shapes emerge.
A cot.
Blankets rotted into dirt.
A broken lantern.
A pair of boots.
And in the far corner—
A depression in the earth.
Small.
Round.
Kneeling.
And beside it—
Another.
Larger.
Sitting.
Watching.

This wasn't a hiding place.

It was a vigil.

Someone stayed.

Something Papa never spoke of.

I kneel.

My hand sinks into loose soil.

And then—

Fabric.

Plaid.

Stiff with age.

A man's sleeve.

"This isn't Tommy's," I whisper.

Dara's breath shatters. "Then whose—"

I already know.

Papa's.

The one he wore the night he ran through the woods.

The one he said tore on a fence.

It didn't.

It tore here.

While he held a dying boy.

The darkness shifts.

A shape sits up.

Broad-shouldered.

Human.

Head bowed.

Not hunting.

Not hostile.

Just… spent.

A sigh moves through the room—older than grief.

"…I tried."

Louis collapses into me—grief, relief, recognition.

Dara sobs. "PaPa…?"
The shadow lifts one hand—not to stop her.
To protect her.
I kneel fully.
"Papa," I whisper.
"…finish it, Claire."
The house shudders.
Outside, the tall figure slams against the siding.
Tommy flickers.
Louis presses me inward—*now*.
The Quiet gathers—not force, not fear.
Alignment.
Everything else holds still.
The tall figure freezes.
Papa bows his head.
Tommy waits.
And from the dirt, the memory, the boy, the man—
one word rises.
Steady.
Certain.
"Claire. Now."

The house holds its breath after the whisper.

Claire—now.

Papa's shadow leans forward, not threatening—pleading. The fabric of his shirt hangs from my hands, heavy with soil, heavy with what he couldn't carry out of this room.

Louis presses into my spine, steady and warm, but weaker than before. Whatever kept him from entering this room is draining him by the second. This space doesn't belong to him—it echoes with someone else's final moment.

Dara stands in the doorway, one hand braced against the frame as if the wood itself is shifting beneath her. She doesn't try to follow.

She can't.

"Claire…" Her voice breaks. "Be careful."

I kneel beside Papa's shadow.

Not close enough to touch him. Just close enough to listen.

"What do I have to finish?" I whisper.

The shadow lifts its head. The shape of his face flickers—young, then old, then caught between the years of guilt and the moment everything changed.

His voice is barely sound.

"He wasn't taken," he says. "I let go."

Something in my chest tightens.

Papa's silhouette trembles, edges fraying like dust loosening from itself.

"I tried to pull him out," he says. "I held him. I prayed. I begged. And he slipped from my hands."

His gaze drifts toward the depression in the dirt where Tommy knelt. Then to the second indentation—where Papa sat.

Where he stayed.

"I stayed with him," Papa whispers. "I stayed until the end."

Dara covers her mouth. "Papa…"

But he isn't looking at her.

He's looking at me.

"At the moment he passed," Papa says, "the house split. Something old reached through. Something I didn't understand."

The Quiet steadies inside me—not power, not force. Understanding.

"It followed me," he says. "It followed the family."

"Papa," I whisper, "what do I do?"

His shadow leans back, settling as if into the dirt one final time.

"Break the circle."

My pulse stutters. "Tommy's?"

"No."

He lifts one trembling hand toward my chest.

"The one it marked around you before you were born," he says. "Yours."

Louis's warmth jolts behind me—sharp, frightened.

Dara leans farther into the doorway. "Claire—what does that mean?"

Papa's outline flickers, thinning.

"You're the first in the line who can see all of it," he whispers. "Not just the boy. Not just the shadow. The whole shape of what took root here."

The house creaks—deep and low—like something beneath the floor is turning in its sleep.

Papa's voice fades.

"It listens when you breathe," he says. "It bends when you quiet."

"But the circle around you—the one it marked for the next Claire—binds you to it."

Cold spreads through my ribs.

The circle wasn't protection.

It was a claim.

"You break that circle," Papa says, "and you free the boy. You free Louis. You free this house from what followed me."

His shadow collapses inward—edges folding, sinking back into the shape of the floor.

"Papa," I whisper, reaching without touching.

He looks up at me one last time.

"I am so sorry, Claire."

A pause.

"I am so proud."

Then his form dissolves.

The whistle at my neck warms—once, like a heartbeat.

Louis presses into me—desperate now, a final surge of heat.

Behind us, in the other room, Tommy flickers inside the circle of light and shadow, small hands lifting as if waiting to be pulled up.

Dara steadies herself in the doorway.

"Claire… we're with you. But tell us what to do."

I stand.

The earth shifts beneath my boots. The house groans.

And for the first time, I feel all of it—the Quiet, the fear, the pull of the circle etched into my line long before I was born.

I inhale once. Hold. Exhale slow.

The floorboards tremble.

"It's my circle," I say. "My line. My turn to break it."

I step back toward the doorway—toward Tommy, toward Louis, toward what waits in the walls.

And the chapter ends on one sentence:

We end this now.

CHAPTER THIRTY-EIGHT — THE UNMAKING

The floor vibrates under my boots the moment I step out of the back room.

Not shaking. Not warning. Reacting.

Dara stiffens beside the doorway, one hand braced against the wall. Mae is still on the floor in the hall, hands clamped over her ears, eyes squeezed shut as if the sound in the house is too much for her bones.

Louis presses into my spine—hot now, almost burning. The land feels the break forming, and Louis feels everything the land does. He knows what comes next.

Tommy flickers in the circle on the floor, his shape sharpening as if my decision is drawing him forward. His hands lift slightly, palms open.

Waiting.

The tall figure strains against the far wall, limbs jerking at wrong angles, head twisting as if scenting a way back into the room Papa protected.

It can feel the shift. The loosening. The break beginning.

Dara looks at me, voice low and shaking. "Claire… what did Papa mean—*break the circle?*"

I lift the drawing.

The circle pulses—darkening, re-darkening—as if something beneath the ink is pushing to stay alive.

"It's not just a drawing," I whisper. "It's a boundary. A mark. A claim."

Mae sobs softly. "On Tommy?"

"No."

I meet her gaze.

"On me."

Louis steadies me with a surge of warmth that spreads up my spine, across my shoulders. A brace. A reminder.

I'm not alone in this.

The tall figure stops twisting.

Its head turns toward me.

Slow. Deliberate.

Like it finally understands what I'm about to do.

Dara grabs my wrist. "Claire—don't move unless you're sure—"

"I am."

I kneel beside the circle where Tommy crouched. His outline trembles, thin and unsteady, like a wick burned nearly through.

"Tommy," I whisper, "I'm going to undo what tied you here. Are you ready?"

His head lifts.

Those pale, waterwashed eyes fix on me—not pleading, not afraid.

Recognizing.

He nods once.

Louis pulses behind me—

Go.

Dara tightens her grip. "Claire… hurry. That thing is watching every breath you take."

I hold the drawing over the floor.

My thumb hovers at the edge of the circle.

The tall figure lunges—

SLAM.

The wall cracks.

Mae screams.

Dara shoves closer. "Claire—NOW."

I inhale. Hold. Exhale slow.

The Quiet folds through me—deep, certain.

The ink trembles.

Tommy's shadow stiffens, bracing.

The tall figure claws at the wall, unable to cross the threshold, its limbs jerking wildly as if something inside it is tearing itself apart.

Louis presses heat into my ribs—

Break it.

I press my thumb to the circle.

Not hard. Not violent. Just enough.

A sound splits the air—

paper tearing, wood sighing, earth shifting.

The circle cracks down the middle.

Tommy's outline erupts in a burst of soft white light—

not blinding, not painful—

releasing.

The tall figure shrieks without a mouth—a hollow, furious sound that rattles the windows.

Mae drops to her knees.

Dara shields her face.

Louis surges into me—warm, relieved, suddenly lighter—

But Tommy—

He stands.

Truly stands.

His form is still thin, still wrong in places, but clearer than it has ever been.

His hands fall to his sides.

He looks at me—

free.

Untethered from what hunted him. Untethered from the piece of my bloodline that carried the mark.

But the tall figure doesn't fall back.

It doesn't fade.

It turns.

Slowly.

Toward me.

Dara's voice fractures. "Claire… why is it looking at *you*?"

I swallow.

"Because I broke its claim."

The circle bound my line to its hunger. Breaking it starves what's been feeding on us for generations.

The tall figure takes one step toward us—long, rattling, furious.

Louis shoves every ounce of warmth into my back—bracing, shielding, screaming without sound.

The house groans under the weight of what we've changed.

Tommy lifts one small hand—pointing again.

Not to the drawing. Not to the corner.

To me.

And the chapter ends as Dara whispers what all of us suddenly understand:

"Claire… it's coming for you now."

Without Tommy's circle to hold it, it needs a new anchor.

And I'm the one who broke its chain.

222

The tall figure takes another step.

The floor bows under its weight, boards groaning like something beneath them wants out. Louis slams warmth into my spine—urgent, frantic—his warning a pulse that lands directly in my ribs.

Dara grabs my arm. "Claire—MOVE."

But I can't yet.

Tommy hasn't.

He stands just outside the broken circle, his outline thin but steady, eyes lifting toward the tall shadow like he's seeing it without fear for the first time.

"Tommy," I whisper. "Go to Louis. Stay with him."

He doesn't.

He steps closer to me.

Louis pushes harder—

No—Claire—behind you—

The house lurches.

Dust shakes loose from the ceiling. Windows rattle in their frames. Mae crawls backward against the hallway wall, crying into her hands.

The tall figure tilts its head toward me with a long, splintering snap.

Dara swings in front of me. "Claire—you're not doing this alone—"

But she can't shield me from something not fully here.

The tall figure leans forward—

—and the wall behind it cracks straight up the plaster, splitting like a seam torn open by hands too strong.

A hollow wind pulls through the house.

Floorboards rise. Nails lift. The air folds inward toward it.

Louis slams heat into me so suddenly I gasp.

His message is clear:

Stay standing. Stay centered. Stay you.

Tommy takes another small step until he's beside my leg, his cold outline brushing my hand.

The tall figure reaches toward us.

Not to grab.

To breach.

Dara screams, "Claire—QUIET IT!"

I draw a breath—deep, steady—the way I did without knowing when I was a child. The way I've always done to still a room, to still myself, to change the shape of air.

The Quiet gathers—

not a weapon, not a shield—

a boundary.

A line drawn through breath. The kind only my bloodline can make.

Louis braces every bone in my spine.

I exhale.

Slow. Even. Directed.

The tall figure jerks back as if struck, limbs snapping outward like they're caught in a current it can't control.

The breach collapses—

walls slamming shut, floor flattening, air snapping clean for a single breath.

Dara covers her head. "Claire—KEEP GOING!"

She can see it. She can't touch it.

Only I can change what it bound.

But the tall figure isn't gone.

It hovers against the far wall—flattened, stretched, furious—its shape vibrating in and out of the plaster like it's trying to tear itself fully through.

The Quiet tightens around me, coiling through my lungs, down my arms, out to my fingertips.

The room bends with the pressure.

Louis strains behind me, heat flickering—

I'm here—but fading—Claire—

Tommy lifts his hand toward the tall figure.

A small, steady gesture.

A refusal.

A boy telling the dark it no longer owns him.

The tall figure shrieks—soundless but violent—shuddering against the wall.

The house bows inward.

Dara grips the doorway. "Claire—if this thing gets through—"

"I know."

I inhale again.

The Quiet pulls deeper.

Calmer.

Older than fear.

The tall figure presses harder—

cracking plaster, splitting boards, forcing itself through one stretched limb at a time.

Louis's warmth flares—painfully bright.

Every inch the breach closes costs him. He's tied to the land's strain.

Claire—now—finish it—

I exhale with everything I have—

not to push, not to destroy,

but to undo the line it carved through my family.

The Quiet releases like a slow, rolling wave.

The tall figure convulses, collapsing inward, folding like a shadow being peeled from the wall.

The breach seals.

The house settles with a deep, exhausted groan.

And the tall figure—

is gone.

For the first time in decades, the air in the room does not hold its weight.

Tommy lowers his hand.

Louis's warmth flickers—soft now, relieved—

free.

Dara sinks to her knees. "Oh my lands… Claire…"

Mae crawls forward, shaking. "Is it over? Claire—please—tell me it's over."

I look at Tommy.

He turns his face toward me—

and for the first time, his shape isn't fear.

It's release.

"It's over," I breathe.

But Louis presses into me, faint now—

Not yet—almost—one last thing—

And the chapter closes on his final whisper pulsing into my bones:

Take him home.

Not Louis. Not Papa.

Tommy.

CHAPTER FORTY — THE WALK OUT

The house settles into a silence so complete it feels unnatural.

Not empty. Not relieved. Just… quiet.

Tommy stands beside me, faint but whole enough that his outline no longer flickers. His hands hang loosely at his sides, palms open—like a child who has finally stopped bracing for impact.

Louis presses into my spine, but the heat is thin now. Unsteady.

He held on as long as Tommy needed him. And now the boy has finally let go.

He's fading.

Dara pushes up from her knees, wiping her face with the back of her sleeve. "Claire—are you okay?"

Mae crawls forward on trembling hands. "Is Tommy—? Can he… leave?"

I look down at him.

He meets my eyes—those pale, washed-out eyes steady now, no longer clouded with panic.

He nods once.

Louis pulses faintly—

Take him home.

I offer Tommy my hand.

He doesn't take it.

He simply stands close enough that I feel a cool ripple across my skin, like mist off a lake at dawn.

Dara steps into the hall, giving us room. Mae presses herself against the far wall, shaking but watching.

I lead Tommy toward the doorway.

The boards under our feet don't groan anymore.

They accept our steps.

Every shift of the house feels lighter, as if some weight in the wood itself has been lifted.

Tommy pauses at the threshold where the tall figure once reached for him.

He looks up at me—then at the place where the wall cracked and healed.

"It's gone," I whisper.

His shoulders loosen.

The smallest, faintest sigh escapes him.

We walk the hallway slowly, past the places where he once ran and hid, past the rooms where he disappeared into memory and dread.

As we pass the crawl gap, Louis's warmth flickers again—

soft. proud. tired.

Dara whispers, "Claire… Louis doesn't feel strong. Is he okay?"

"I don't know," I say.

My voice is steady. My hands are not.

Tommy reaches the front door first.

He stops.

The night outside is still, windless. The woods beyond are dark but no longer watchful. The lake is quiet. The air is cold in a natural way—not the spoiled cold that seeped from the room.

Mae pulls herself upright, wiping her face. "Where does he go?"

Before I can answer, Tommy turns.

He looks up the staircase—the one with the broken railing hinge he hid. He looks toward the kitchen—the last place he was whole.

Then he looks back at me.

Louis's warmth steadies once more—

Let him choose.

I kneel.

"You don't have to stay," I say softly. "You're not trapped here anymore. You can go anywhere you want."

Tommy lifts one finger—

toward the front door.

I nod.

"Okay."

Dara wipes her eyes. "Sweet boy…"

Mae whispers, "Claire… walk with him."

I do.

I open the door slowly, letting the night air spill inside.

It feels clean.

Tommy steps onto the porch.

Louis follows us, his warmth thinning with each step, like a lantern guttering toward dawn.

Tommy turns toward the yard.

The woods rustle. A breeze lifts, gentle—as if greeting him.

He takes one step into the night.

Then another.

His outline flickers—

not from fear, but from release.

Louis's warmth trembles in my ribs—

I'm right behind him—almost done—almost free—

Tommy pauses at the edge of the yard.

He turns back one last time.

Raises his hand.

A small wave—a gesture he never finished in life.

And then he dissolves like dust caught in morning light.

Gone.

Not taken.

Gone home.

Louis presses one final burst of warmth into my chest—

Thank you.

The warmth fades.

The Quiet locks into place, and the house stops fighting itself.

Mae sobs softly.

Dara steps beside me, placing a shaking hand on my shoulder.

The front door hangs open, letting the night breathe through it.

I whisper the truth aloud—more to the land than to them.

"It's over."

But the chapter ends with the smallest tremor beneath my boots—

not dangerous, not dark,

just… waiting.

Because the house isn't finished speaking yet.

It never was only about Tommy.

CHAPTER FORTY-ONE—THE HOUSE SPEAKS

The night settles around us, cool and clean—the way winter air is supposed to feel. Not heavy. Not haunted. Just cold.

Behind me, the house gives one last gentle groan, the sound wood makes when it finally stops bracing against something unseen.

Dara steps beside me on the porch, arms crossed tight. Mae wipes her face with both hands, sniffling.

For a moment, none of us move.

The wind lifts across the yard—not strong, just present—rustling the dead leaves like a long-held breath finally let out.

I step back toward the doorway.

Louis doesn't follow.

The warmth that once pressed into my spine is gone—not violently, not in fear—but the way a lantern goes dark once its work is finished. And I know what it means.

Dara sees the shift in my expression. "Claire? Is he…?"

I swallow. "He's free."

Mae leans against the porch railing, crying quietly. "I can't believe any of this was real."

Dara squeezes her eyes shut, then opens them again. "The house feels… different. Doesn't it?"

It does.

The moment I cross the threshold back inside, I feel it in the walls—a settling, a softening, the way a grieving person exhales after finally speaking the truth.

The dark corners aren't watching anymore. The air isn't waiting.

I walk down the hall—the same hall where Tommy flickered, where Louis steadied me, where the tall shadow strained against the plaster.

Every step feels lighter.

Dara and Mae follow close behind.

When I reach the room where the circle broke, the floor is still warped from decades of pressure. But the shadows are gone.

Not thinned gone. Gone.

The air is just air.

Mae whispers, "Do you think Papa is still here?"

I shake my head. "No. He stayed until the boy was safe. That was his vigil. And it's done."

Dara covers her mouth with one trembling hand. "He wasn't holding on to us. He was trapped in his regret."

"He's not trapped anymore," I say.

We move toward the back room—the one Papa never allowed anyone to enter. The smell of soil still lingers, but the heaviness is gone.

I kneel where his outline once rose from the dirt.

Nothing stirs. No voice. No whisper.

Just earth.

I touch the place where his shirt lay—now only loose soil beneath my palm.

"Thank you," I whisper.

Not to summon him. Just to honor him.

The house answers with a soft creak in the beams above us—gentle, almost warm.

Mae steps forward hesitantly. "So… what happens now?"

I stand slowly, brushing dirt from my hands. "Now we leave," I say.

And this house finally belongs to no one.

Dara looks around, her eyes glassy but relieved. "Claire… this doesn't feel like the end of something bad. It feels like the end of something sad."

She's right.

The fear is gone. But the grief remains—raw, old, and finally allowed to breathe.

I lead us back toward the front door.

As I step onto the porch again, the floorboards sigh beneath my boots—a real sigh this time. Not a warning. Not a cry.

Just release.

The wind moves across the yard. The lake shifts in the distance.

Dara pulls the door closed behind us.

The house doesn't settle.

It rebalances—old weight gone, new truth resting where it belongs.

And whatever speaks next won't be borrowed from the dead.

It will be ours.

CHAPTER FORTY-TWO—THE LEAVING

The cold air outside feels lighter than it should. Not joyful. Not cleansing. Just real. Normal.

Mae steps down the porch first, shivering in her coat though the wind is barely there. She keeps wiping her eyes, like the tears won't quite settle.

Dara lingers in the doorway behind us, one hand resting on the frame as if the house might pull her back in.

It doesn't.

She exhales slowly—the way someone does after a long drive or a long argument. Tired. Relieved. Unsure.

None of us speak as we walk toward the gravel drive.

The sky has thinned to that pale gray-blue that comes right before dawn. The trees are still enough that every crunch of our boots sounds too loud.

Louis is gone. But the space he filled still feels warm at my back, like the echo of a touch that hasn't quite decided to leave.

Mae reaches the cars first. Mom and Dad are already tucked into the cold interior when she turns to me.

"Can we… go home now?"

"Yes," I say.

Dara stands a few feet away near her own car. She doesn't step toward me. She's caught in that awkward space people fall into after sharing something enormous—when there's no script for what comes next.

She glances at me.

Not defiant. Not apologetic. Just… there.

For a moment we stand in a quiet shaped by everything we've been through—and everything we'll never be for each other.

Dara clears her throat.

"Well."

Her voice is rough, almost embarrassed by its own softness.

"We did it."

I nod. "We did."

She shrugs slightly, eyes on the gravel. "Didn't think we could."

"We didn't have a choice."

A small, almost-smile flickers at her mouth.

"Guess that's true."

We stand there in a silence that isn't warm and isn't cold—just honest. A kind of truth we've never managed to offer each other before.

Mae watches us carefully, like she's afraid one wrong word might tip the balance.

But nothing tips. Nothing breaks.

After a long breath, Dara says quietly, "Take care of Hallie. Mae. And yourself."

"I will."

She nods once. Hard.

"Good."

She turns toward her car.

Pauses.

Looks back over her shoulder—not searching for connection, not expecting anything—just acknowledging the moment for what it was.

"Claire…"

Her voice is steadier now.

"I'm glad Hallie got to know me. Before… everything fell apart again."

My throat tightens, but I don't look away.

"Me too."

It's the closest either of us will come to forgiveness. Or to asking for it.

Dara blinks quickly, then gets into her car.

The engine turns over.

Headlights sweep across the yard.

She backs down the long drive without another word.

Mae watches the taillights disappear between the trees.

"Do you think you'll talk to her again?"

"I don't know," I say.

And the truth is, that answer feels right.

Not hopeful. Not hopeless. Just honest.

Mae nods, accepting it.

The gravel settles.

Behind us, the house is silent—truly silent. Not waiting. Not grieving.

I open the driver's door.

"Come on, Mae," I say gently. "Let's go home."

She nods and climbs in.

I take one last look toward the house.

No shadows in the windows. No shapes in the yard. No cold behind my ribs.

Just a place.

A place that finally let go.

I start the car.

The engine catches.
And we drive away.

CHAPTER FORTY-THREE—THE LAST LIGHT

The drive home is still in a way that feels earned.

Mae leans against the window, her breath fogging the glass in small, steady bursts. My parents sit in the back, speaking only in soft murmurs—the kind families use after a long day of emotion they don't yet have words for.

No one mentions the house. No one needs to.

By the time we reach my neighborhood, the sun is slipping behind the trees, turning the sky a soft peach that makes everything look gentler than it felt the night before.

Sam is waiting in the doorway when we pull in.

He always looks steady to me—but tonight he looks like home.

He meets me at the car before I can grab my bag.

"You're home, Kitten. You okay?"

It isn't the kind of question you answer with a story. Just a truth.

"I'm here," I say.

He kisses the top of my head and pulls me close for a moment longer than usual.

Mae stretches slowly, eyes tired but clearer than they've been in days. She gives Sam a small wave as she heads inside with my parents.

When I step through the door, the house hums with a different kind of quiet—warm, lived-in.

Hallie looks up from the couch, wrapped in a blanket, her hair messy from sleep she tried not to show.

"Mom?" she asks softly.

"I'm okay," I tell her.

She nods once—the kind of nod that comes from trust—and settles back beside my dad, her hand slipping into his like she's anchoring him back into the world.

My black cat, Echo, appears instantly, winding between my legs, purring with a fullness that feels like relief. Like recognition. Like welcome.

I run my hand along his back and feel something unclench inside me.

We move around each other in the softness of evening—Sam making tea without asking if I want one, Mae settling into the armchair with my mom, Hallie yawning and pulling her blanket tighter.

Normal.

My normal.

Later, after everyone drifts to their rooms, I slip beneath my blankets. The air is still. The dark is ordinary. My cat curls into the hollow behind my knees.

For a long moment, I listen.

Not for footsteps. Not for whispers. Not for anything reaching from somewhere it shouldn't.

Just… listening.

Waiting for the Quiet inside me to press. To warn.

But it doesn't.

It lies still—calm, folded deep inside me like a breath that's finally found its place.

Sam slides into bed beside me, brushing my hair back with the side of his hand.

"Try to sleep, kitten."

"I will," I whisper.

And I do.

Not because everything is fixed. Not because the past is gone.

But because, for the first time in a long time, the quiet inside me is mine— not the house's, not the land's, not the shadows'.

Just mine.

The last thing I feel before sleep takes me is the soft weight of my cat at my feet, warm and ordinary.

And the last thought I have is simple:

My Quiet is quiet.

WHAT IS ALLOWED

Dara notices the change on a morning that doesn't announce itself.

No weather. No pressure in the air. Just the absence of something that used to complicate the room.

She stands at the sink in her own house, hands submerged in water she's forgotten to turn off. The sound has gone thin, almost polite. She shuts the tap and lets the silence settle into place.

It isn't relief.

Relief implies struggle.

This is alignment.

She dries her hands carefully, one finger at a time, pressing the towel into the grooves of her skin as if confirming boundaries. The mirror above the sink holds her reflection steady. No distortion. No flicker. She looks exactly as she expects to.

That's how she knows.

Whatever closed did not close *her*.

The farm is already receding — not into memory, not into guilt, but into irrelevance. It served its function. It drew the shape of a boundary and then withdrew from the work of enforcing it.

Dara respects that.

Systems that know when to stop are more interesting than ones that don't.

She moves through the house with the efficiency of someone who has waited long enough to begin. Lights switched on. Switched off. Nothing ceremonial. She isn't marking time — she's confirming access.

Her phone rests on the counter. No new messages. No missed calls.

She expected that.

Claire has always been reliable about restraint. Dara had bet on it. The line would be drawn. It would hold. It always does when it's held by someone who believes in consequence more than outcome.

That's the difference between them.

Dara doesn't resent the line.

She appreciates the clarity.

Before, there was always the question of interference — a quiet pressure she could feel even when it wasn't being used. The possibility of correction was enough to complicate things. It made outcomes imprecise.

Now that ambiguity is gone.

She pours herself coffee and sits at the table by the window, her back straight, her posture unguarded. The neighborhood moves through its small rhythms outside — a garbage truck, a jogger, a dog pulling against a leash.

Ordinary life doesn't notice thresholds.

That has always been its weakness.

Dara sips, thinking not about what she wants, but about what no longer resists her wanting it. There is a pleasure in limitation when it clarifies direction. Too much permission muddies intention. Too many eyes turn necessity into performance.

There will be no performance now.

She doesn't rush.

Rushing is for people who fear reconsideration.

Dara has never worried about changing her mind. She knows exactly what remains once pretense is stripped away. What others call cruelty, she experiences as precision. What they call harm, she recognizes as coherence.

She finishes her coffee and rinses the cup, placing it upside down to dry. The house around her feels neutral. Not watchful. Not concerned.

That's new.

Before, there had been a kind of ambient accounting — a sense that actions registered somewhere outside the room, even if nothing came of them immediately. She hadn't minded. She understood the purpose. But its absence sharpens the present.

This is what being unobserved feels like when it's deserved.

She thinks briefly of Claire — not with anger or tenderness, but with something close to respect. It takes discipline to stop where you could continue. To accept containment when no one is forcing it on you.

Claire will live well inside her choices.

That has never been the problem.

Dara steps outside and breathes in the morning. The air offers nothing back. No signals. No invitations. Just space and permission.

She smiles then — not widely, not for effect. A private expression, barely there.

The world hasn't gone quiet.

It's gone clear.

Whatever happens next will not be accidental. There will be no misunderstanding, no shared illusion of innocence. The line has made that impossible.

And that, more than anything, feels like freedom.

Dara turns and goes back inside.

There is work to be done.

I wake before dawn, the room still wrapped in that soft blue-gray that comes only in winter.

Sam sleeps beside me, breath even, one arm curled over his head to block the light the way it always does when he finally drifts deep. He's a light sleeper, so I ease the blankets back and slip from the bed slowly, careful not to shift the mattress.

The house is warm. Normal. Still.

My office area sits in the far corner of our bedroom—shelving, a small desk, a scatter of notebooks and folders I'm always promising myself I'll organize. Something pulls me toward it.

Not urgency. Not the Quiet.

Just the gentle tug of sentiment—the kind that follows long days and leaves its mark quietly.

I move across the room, watching the floorboards, avoiding the one plank that creaks near the dresser. When I reach the shelves, I start sifting through a few stacks, meaning only to straighten them.

That's when I see it.

A simple envelope. Soft around the edges. My mother's handwriting on the front.

I forgot I even had it.

I pick it up carefully, glance once toward the bed. Sam hasn't stirred. I ease the flap open, mindful of every sound in the stillness.

Inside is a single folded sheet of paper.

Handwritten. Old. The steady cursive of a woman who knew the stories of the land before any of us were ready to hear them.

I unfold it slowly.

The paper smells faintly of cedar and something older—like a trunk that's been closed too long.

The letter isn't long. Most of it is ordinary family recollection: a farm, children, a memory of someone braiding her hair on summer porches.

And then—halfway down the page—one line catches.

A name I don't recognize. French-inflected. Curled handwriting.

Beneath it, a place written smaller, less certain:

New Orleans.

I read it twice. Then once more.

A relative sent south to stay with her mother's people. A quiet suggestion that what runs through our line didn't begin in Missouri at all. A note—careful, almost apologetic—that the family had roots farther south, in one of the old French districts the writer could no longer name with confidence.

The Quiet inside me stirs once.

Not a warning. Not even a pulse.

Just recognition. The way something familiar answers without asking why.

I fold the letter carefully, tracing the crease with my thumb. The house remains silent. Sam is still asleep. The world feels small and steady again.

But something in the ink lingers.

Something older than the farm. Something that precedes it.

I slide the letter back into its envelope and hold it in both hands.

Dawn lifts faintly at the edge of the curtains, softening the room around me.

Missouri was only the beginning.

Somewhere beyond the river and the winter fields—past what I know how to name—another truth is waiting.

Quietly. Patiently.